THE MISGIVINGS ABOUT MISS PRUDENCE

SCHOOL OF CHARM #4

MAGGIE DALLEN

1

There was nothing mysterious about Miss Prudence Pottermouth. With Prudence, what one saw was what one got.

For the most part.

She had precisely two secrets which she kept from her friends at Miss Grayson's School of Charm, a finishing school for refined young ladies. Or, as her friend Louisa put it—a finishing school for young ladies whose guardians knew not what to do with them.

She wasn't wrong.

For Prudence, in particular, that description had always seemed acutely apt. She'd spent the better part of two years at this school, alongside her best friend Delilah and the other girls, and it was precisely because she was not wanted anywhere else.

That was her first secret. Although, considering Louisa, Addie, and Delilah had been at her side earlier today when she'd eavesdropped on Miss Grayson's conversation with her great aunt, she supposed that secret was out.

"But surely Miss Pottermouth's parents—" Miss Grayson had started.

"Her parents neither know nor care what that girl is doing," Aunt Eleanor had snapped.

Prudence winced at the memory of those words. True, to be certain, but still unpleasant to hear. Even more so when she'd glanced over to find her friends eyeing her with varying degrees of sympathy and pity.

And that right there was why she'd kept her unwanted status a secret. She was not one to be pitied. She'd been given every advantage as a child, thanks to her great aunt's management. And her time at Miss Grayson's had given her the feeling of home she'd never known she'd been missing. Because of this, it was only natural that she should be feeling a bit emotional about leaving.

Prudence frowned down at the bag she was packing with her belongings.

This feeling was definitely only natural—but it was still unwelcome.

"I am certain she won't keep you away from us for long," Delilah said reassuringly as she watched Prudence pack her life away. Well, she'd said it as reassuringly as a lady like Delilah was able. Which was to say, not very reassuringly at all.

Though her recent adventures and her newly formed engagement with Lord Rupert had softened Prudence's friend a little, Delilah could not quite shake a lifetime of cool arrogance and that haughty demeanor.

Prudence gave her friend a small smile. She didn't mind Delilah's standoffish ways. She never had. Perhaps because she'd always understood that beneath that icy hauture was a heart of gold.

Well, perhaps not *gold*. But not the cold lump of ice she pretended to have, either.

"Yes, I'm sure you'll be back before we know it," Addie said.

Ever the optimist, Addie was giving her an encouraging smile that had the opposite effect. Rather than making her feel better, the flicker of pity she caught in the other girl's eyes made her want to slam her trunk shut and pull her bag of sweets out of its hiding spot.

That was her second secret. Her private pleasure. Her only vice.

"I still don't understand what your great aunt was so upset about," Louisa said.

Leave it to Louisa to bring up the more awkward aspect of the conversation they'd overheard.

"I thought she made herself quite clear." Delilah's voice dripped with anger.

Delilah might have had her faults, but as a friend she was utterly devoted. Prudence suspected she'd been more upset than anyone at the way her great aunt had spoken about her...and her horrid performance.

Prudence struggled to be a mediocre musician at the best of times, but under her great aunt's terrifying, watchful stare...

She'd been dreadful.

"I had no idea anyone could get so worked up over a recital," Addie murmured.

Prudence winced. And then she gave into the overwhelming need for sugar and pulled out her secret stash, popping a lemon sweet into her mouth as she suffered through another wave of embarrassment.

"Just because you do not have an ear for music—" Addie began.

"No ear for music?" Louisa laughed. "That's an understatement, wouldn't you say?"

Prudence did not have to look to know that Louisa's

sudden silence was in response to the warning glare she was no doubt getting from Delilah and the more gentle shake of a head from Addie.

Louisa had a knack for speaking out of turn, but right now Prudence couldn't quite bring herself to scold her friend for that fault.

Not when her own flaw had been so glaringly brought into the light.

"Whether she's a musical prodigy or not is beside the point," Delilah said. "What matters is that her aunt ought not to speak of her like that."

"That is very true," Addie said. "She was remarkably uncharitable, especially considering how well Prudence has mastered every other lesson."

Delilah turned to Prudence with barely concealed rage. "You ought not listen to her, Pru. Your aunt is a beast," she said. "She makes my stepmother look saintly."

Louisa snickered at that. Even Addie smiled.

Prudence sighed, rolling her eyes at her friend's exaggeration. In the months since Delilah's adventure, she'd become more and more fond of finding the humor in her story, which was like something straight out of a gothic romance.

She supposed Delilah's good humor on the topic was Lord Rupert's influence. The charming gentleman who'd saved Delilah from her stepmother's evil plans had softened Delilah considerably, bringing out her natural warmth and wit.

Prudence pursed her lips as she scowled at her friend. "Really, Dee. Your stepmother planned to murder you. I hardly think it is fair to compare Aunt Eleanor to that wicked woman."

Delilah shrugged, unapologetic. "She shouldn't be allowed to talk about you like that."

"What does she expect?" Addie asked, her voice rising in a

rare show of outrage. "Does she think you have to be perfect in order to find a good match?"

Yes. Prudence bit her tongue to keep from answering what was obviously a rhetorical question. But truly, yes, that was exactly what her aunt expected.

"But Prudence *is* perfect, Addie," Louisa interjected with a mischievous little grin. "She's told us so herself any number of times, haven't you, Pru?"

"Louisa," Addie sighed.

"Not now, Louisa," Delilah snapped.

Prudence didn't mind her teasing. This was the way it had always been between her and Louisa ever since the other girl joined her as a student at this school. While she considered Louisa a friend, the outspoken redhead was in every way her opposite. Prudence disapproved of just about everything Louisa did and Louisa found Prudence to be unbearably sanctimonious. They'd butted heads since day one and while they cared about one another, their relationship was far more akin to siblings who teased and squabbled than true friends.

Or at least, that was what Prudence suspected. She had no siblings so she had nothing to compare it to.

"She knows I'm teasing," Louisa protested. "Don't you, Pru?"

"Of course I do," Prudence said with a weary sigh. "But you must mind your manners, Louisa, if you're ever going to be a respectable marchioness."

Louisa's grin was filled with joy at the mere mention of her upcoming marriage. "Don't you worry about me, Pru. Tumberland loves me just the way I am."

Prudence rolled her eyes. Out of habit she looked to Delilah to share in her distaste for Louisa and Addie's sappy sighs, but Delilah was too busy smiling vapidly just like the others.

Prudence sighed and reached for another sweet.

Perhaps it was for the best that Aunt Eleanor was bringing her back to her country estate. Ever since Delilah had gone and fallen in love, Prudence had become the odd woman out.

While the rest of her friends prattled on about upcoming weddings and talked of true love and destiny, Prudence sat by and listened and tried not to lose the contents of her stomach at the sickening romantic drivel.

Romance was just another word for selfish decisions, as far as Prudence was concerned. Love was just a fantasy, ephemeral and weak. Neither romance nor love ought to take the place of reason when it came to making life-altering decisions.

But she knew better than to try and convince her friends of this. They would look at her like she'd gone mad and then return to their plans for wedded bliss.

She made a rather unattractive and cynical snorting sound as she sucked on her candy.

Yes, it was definitely for the best that she was leaving. This sense of homesickness would pass once the school was out of sight, and her aunt, while perhaps a bit too harsh with her criticisms, had not been wrong.

While Miss Grayson and the other tutors at this school had helped her refine her skills, she was still a failure when it came to music.

To Addie's point, her great aunt expected Prudence to be perfect. And while that might seem unfair to Addie and the others, it was the way she'd been raised.

Her every decision and choice were with the one aim of becoming the perfect wife for the eldest Mr. Benedict, the son of a wealthy merchant who her great aunt had forged an understanding with when she was only a child.

It might not have been such a fine match as Louisa had

made, or Addie, or even Delilah, but it was a good match, considering that her parents had been a disgrace amongst the ton. Her great aunt might have been a dowager duchess, but Prudence was her youngest sister's youngest daughter's only daughter.

The only reason she had any prospects at all was due to her great aunt's sense of obligation. She ought to be grateful that her aunt had found her a marriage prospect at all.

She had not yet had the pleasure of meeting Mr. Benedict's acquaintance, but her aunt assured her he was the perfect match, and for him she was to be perfect as well. Anything less would be disrespectful to the arrangement.

Oh, it was not a formal arrangement, but everyone knew it would come to pass. Just as soon as she overcame her last fault. Her fatal flaw.

Her eyes narrowed as she shoved the bag of sweets out of sight to avoid further temptation.

Silly music. She despised the topic. Hated balls for the mere fact that they almost always included it—dancing would be rather difficult without it, she supposed.

And yet, she still resented it. She resented even more those people for whom it came so easily. Which, right now, seemed to include every other person in this room.

"In all seriousness, though, Pru..." Louisa interrupted her rapidly rising frustration. "Your aunt really should not talk about you like that. As though you're just some...some—"

Prudence snapped the trunk shut with a loud click to cut off Louisa's statement. She did not wish to hear how it would end.

It was bad enough that her friends had overheard that dreadful, humiliating lecture on Prudence's stubborn flaws and Miss Grayson's inability to fix them. But to see Louisa, of all people, feeling sorry for her...

It was too much.

"That is enough," she said, her chin held high as she turned to face her irritating but well-intentioned friends. "We should not have been eavesdropping in the first place."

To a one, her friends' expressions fell. The camaraderie of the moment seemed to shift as she spoke. She could see them going on the defensive, as they always did when she became "unbearably sanctimonious" or "a self-righteous know-it-all," as Louisa put it.

She tilted her chin higher, some of her hurt emotions fading behind the familiar mask of indifference. "It's my own fault for listening in on a conversation that was not meant for my ears."

"But—"

"We should never have eavesdropped," she said again, firmer this time to override Addie's protest. "I should never have let you talk me into it."

This last part was aimed at Louisa directly, and her friend flinched. "I didn't force you," she muttered, but her gaze fell with a guilty look.

"Now then," Prudence said with a calm she did not feel. "If you'll excuse me. I must finish packing if I am to leave for my aunt's home in the morning."

* * *

THE CARRIAGE RIDE was both a blessing and curse.

It was with relief that Prudence lost herself to the rhythmic clopping of the horses' hooves as the school and London were left behind her.

She'd never been fond of farewells. Or the emotions that tended to come with them. So it was a relief to have that behind her. The ache she felt would fade, of that she was certain.

She'd learned from experience that the pain of loss and

leaving was short-lived. One merely had to bear with it for a while.

She dug into her reticule and pulled out one of the last of her sweets. Experience had also taught her that sweets helped to ease any pain.

"Put that away, girl. We have enough to overcome before Mr. Benedict arrives without adding your excessive weight to the mix."

Prudence dropped the treat quickly, her cheeks burning with embarrassment. While she'd never been as svelte as her friends at the finishing school, she'd never felt so very overweight as she did at this precise moment with her stick-thin elderly aunt eyeing her like she was an eyesore who ought not to be admitted into good company.

She folded her hands in her lap, focusing on the view outside the carriage rather than the blow to her pride. It wasn't until she'd watched trees whip past her and her breathing evened that her great aunt's words truly registered.

When they did, they left her winded. "Mr. Benedict is coming to visit?"

Her great aunt blinked at her from behind her spectacles as if eyeing something odious. "Of course. He and his uncle, Sir William. Why else do you think I came for you?"

Why else, indeed? Surely not for the pleasure of my company.

She sniffed, brushing aside the bitter thought.

Sarcasm was a bad habit, not one to be indulged. It was merely hostility masquerading as humor. That was what Aunt Eleanor would say.

And she was right.

She was always right.

Waiting until her features were composed and her posture perfect, she ventured once more into the treacherous topic of her would-be fiancé.

The fact that the arrangement had yet to be finalized was still a sensitive topic.

A topic that grew ever more sensitive with each passing year that their engagement was not announced and a wedding date not set.

But then again, Mr. Benedict was a busy man. Her great aunt so often said so.

An exacting man, from what she'd heard. To be honest, she did not know much about the man she was to wed except that her parents and his had once been friends.

Though his parents had presumably stuck around to watch him grow up while hers had cast aside all parental obligations from the day she was born.

They were too in love, you see.

She fought the urge to roll her eyes at the phrase she'd overheard more times than she could count as an adolescent.

Too in love. So very in love. Aren't they so romantic?

Oh yes. Her parents were so very romantic, the sort of love story that gossip mongers loved to whisper about and sigh over even as they condemned the lovers for their improper ways.

A modern-day Romeo and Juliet except that they'd found their happily ever after and left their only child to deal with the ensuing tragedy.

Prudence's mother was supposed to marry another, and by casting aside the man she was meant to marry for the man she'd loved since she was a girl… Well, it was both objectionable and admired among the ladies of the *ton*.

Or so she'd been told. From her great aunt's perspective it was merely objectionable, and Prudence couldn't help but agree.

"It's about time that boy makes this official," her aunt muttered.

Prudence looked up with a start. She'd hardly realized her

aunt was still talking until she smacked her gloves against her palm in a sound that seemed to echo through the small carriage.

"Pardon me?" Prudence said.

"I will have a talk with him and his uncle when they arrive." It seemed as though Prudence was no longer an active part of this conversation.

Young ladies were to be seen and not heard, as her aunt liked to point out. That was always the case when she was speaking to Prudence.

No responses were required or welcome unless they were specifically requested. So she listened quietly now as her great aunt spoke ad nauseum about the insulting way Mr. Benedict had procrastinated on setting a date or formalizing the engagement.

"It's unheard of," Aunt Eleanor said. "It's disrespectful."

No, just humiliating. At this point, it was merely humiliating. Eleanor had to realize what was happening here. Mr. Benedict and his family were waiting to see if a better offer came along.

After all, this arrangement had been discussed when they were mere children and the friendship with her parents had been a solid, dependable thing.

But now a decade had passed and her parents had as little regard for their friends as they had their daughter, allowing even their longest acquaintances to fall by the wayside as they galavanted around the world like gypsies.

While Prudence's dowry was ample and her connections better than most, she was hardly in a class of her own. There were any number of women who had more to recommend themselves and quite honestly Prudence thought Mr. Benedict would be foolish not to consider his options.

A flurry of unease unfurled in her belly at the thought.

It was not that she was so very set on this match. After all, she did not even know the man in question. But her aunt was set on it and that was what mattered.

For, if this fell through...

Well, it wasn't as though there was a queue forming for unwanted, not terribly well connected, plain looking young ladies, now was there?

She shifted as the unpleasant thought was followed by another even more unpleasant sensation.

Fear.

It was fear, plain and simple. All this time she'd taken Mr. Benedict's procrastination as nothing more than a wealthy man's whim. He was not in a rush to marry, so why rush the engagement?

But now...

If her great aunt was worried—and she clearly was—then perhaps she ought to be worried, as well.

"I should never have sent you to that school," her aunt continued. "Miss Grayson clearly allowed you to be as lazy as ever."

"She did not—" Her protest died in her throat under her great aunt's withering glare.

Her throat felt choked under the heat of it.

She hadn't been silly enough to defend herself—nothing she said or did would convince Aunt Eleanor that she was anything other than lazy, fat, and ungrateful. But she couldn't sit by and let Miss Grayson be slandered.

Miss Grayson, who'd been so kind to her. Even during those moments when the others merely tolerated her, Miss Grayson had treated her with love and kindness.

Almost like a mother.

The thought made her lips twitch upwards. Miss Grayson was not even a decade older than her and she had ten times more beauty than Prudence ever could. She hardly fit the role of her mother.

An older sister, perhaps.

Whatever her role, she ought not to have her name or her school in jeopardy merely because Prudence was a failure at music.

"It wasn't Miss Grayson's fault that I haven't mastered music, Aunt," she forced herself to continue despite the wicked glare.

"We'll see about that."

Prudence blinked in surprise at the cryptic comment. "What does that mean?"

"It means I have taken it upon myself to find you a new tutor. One who has a great reputation for making young ladies such as yourself find the discipline necessary to mastering the pianoforte."

Prudence straightened with alarm. Images of harsh instructors from her past came back to haunt her as well as the sting of their ruler when she failed to perform without error.

Which would it be? Or had her aunt found someone even more fearsome for her to learn from?

The thought left her winded with a whole new terror that had nothing to do with the spinster life that loomed ahead of her and everything to do with torturous, painful lessons.

"Lord Damian comes highly recommended."

"Damian?" she repeated without thinking.

"Surely you remember the Marquess of Ainsley's nephew. He's made quite a name for himself as a music tutor among the *ton*." Her eyes narrowed on Prudence with scorn. "He will whip you into shape or you and your hopes of marriage are as good as done for."

She blinked once. Then she blinked again. Shock didn't begin to cover it. Amusement warred with disbelief which battled with incomprehension.

Surely she wasn't talking about *the* Lord Damian.

That man wouldn't know the word discipline if it slapped him across the knuckles.

No, there was only one word that Prudence associated with Damian. And that word...?

Rake.

2

*P*rim, proper, and utterly impossible. Those were the words that came to mind when Damian tried to recall Miss Prudence.

His lips curved into a sneer at the memory of her when they were young. All goody-two-shoes propriety, even as a child. He and his brother and the other neighboring children would be climbing trees and racing across the meadow or wading in the river, but Prudence?

Oh no. She would never.

He rolled his eyes, only dimly aware of his uncle's voice intruding on his admittedly childish thoughts.

He really ought to have overcome his dislike of the neighbor girl, and he might have if she hadn't been the one to get him into trouble at every turn.

A tattletale, through and through.

Even now she was giving him grief and he hadn't seen the girl in years.

"Damian, are you listening?" His uncle's brows were arched so high they nearly reached the older man's thick dark hair, which these last few years had been showing signs of his age as gray edged his temples.

"Er…" *No.* The answer was clearly no, he had not been listening.

His uncle, the Marquess of Ainsley, sank back in his seat with a weary sigh that made him sound decades older than he was.

Or perhaps that was Damian's doing. He seemed to have a special knack for making his uncle sigh with weariness.

"You cannot be serious with this music tutoring business," his uncle said now.

His uncle was a good man. A kind man. Gruff, no doubt, and filled with the sort of old-fashion ideals that made him and all the others of his ilk such a bore to be around. But a good man, nonetheless.

"I am indeed, serious," Damian said with a pleasantness he hadn't quite felt since discovering who his new pupil would be.

Prim and prudish Prudence.

Insufferable little brat.

But, money was money, and her great aunt's money would spend just as well as any others, even if hers would be a good deal more loathsome to earn.

Not that he would ever tell his uncle that.

"Aren't you at all concerned with your future? Your reputation?" His uncle's thick brows were drawn together now in confusion and despair.

"Ah yes, my reputation." Damian smirked. "Perhaps *someone* ought to have thought about that before cutting me off."

Wrong thing to say.

Some said the eyes were the window to the soul. For the marquess, the eyebrows were the window to his mood.

THE MISGIVINGS ABOUT MISS PRUDENCE

When they drew down like this into a fierce glower, it was clear Damian had pushed too far.

"Is that a threat?" his uncle growled. "Is this some sort of childish blackmail, a spoiled child's idea of comeuppance, perhaps?"

Damian shifted in his seat, discomfited by his uncle's sharp tone. "No, of course not."

Not anymore, at least. It had started out that way. Hiring himself out as a music tutor had been a way to thumb his nose at his guardian out of frustration when his funds and life as he knew it had been shut off.

After an admittedly debaucherous stint in London with his friends from school, his uncle had cut off all funds. Rather than tucking his tail between his legs and hurrying home with promises to curtail his revelry and live the life of a pious saint, he'd done the opposite. He'd gone off on his own, determined to make his own way. Tutoring young ladies in music had been a bit of a laugh at first.

He and his chums at the club had joked about how the dimwitted members of society were inviting the rooster into the henhouse. Imagine, paying a gentleman like him to be alone in close quarters with their young and innocent darlings.

But then again, Damian had always excelled at selling himself. His one skill, apart from a knack for music, was to play the role that was expected of him. If an elderly lady in the countryside wanted an upright, studious disciplinarian to teach her great niece the pianoforte, then by golly, he would be the strictest, most serious music instructor the old bat had ever seen.

His uncle sighed again, this time in defeat. "That *is* it, isn't it. You are trying to make a fool of me."

"No, Uncle, I swear it." He leaned forward so his uncle could see that he was in earnest. Damian might have been able to fool the world with his acting, but there was only one person on this earth who could see through all that, and that was the man who'd taken him in as a child and raised him as if he were his own son.

"Uncle, I promise you, I am not trying to make a fool of you." He cleared his throat. "You know I've always been grateful for everything you've done for me."

"Hmph." Despite his huff, Uncle Edward seemed to lose some of his anger with that concession. "Then what do you mean to prove by—"

"I mean to prove that I can make my own way." The moment the disturbingly upstanding words were out of his mouth, Damian had the alarming realization that there was some truth there.

Judging by his uncle's wide-eyed stare, he'd come to the same conclusion. "So it means that much to you then?"

"It does."

Even more alarming? That too was the truth. This whole endeavor had started as a joke. A prank, of sorts, at the very least. But then he'd found that, much to his dismay, he actually liked teaching music.

It helped when the young ladies in question were beautiful, of course. It was very nearly a joy when the girl in question proved to be a flirt. But, above and beyond the divertisement of watching young ladies swoon when he performed for them, there was something else. Something he was loath to name.

Something very similar to...pride.

He shifted uncomfortably again, wishing he was anywhere but here. It was all fine and good to enjoy his new career. It was even better that he'd found some form of pride in what his peers would likely see as a humiliating downgrade in status.

But while it was one thing to feel that way, it was quite another to have to stop and acknowledge the fact.

Intentionally or not, his uncle was rubbing Damian's nose in the fact that he'd gone and found an—oh curse it. He'd found a *work ethic*, plain and simple.

As if he could read his mind, his uncle wore a thoroughly satisfied, completely off putting smile when he next spoke. "In that case, I see I have no choice but to condone this new pastime of yours."

Damian let out a sigh of relief. Not so much because he'd been granted permission—for years now he'd been acting blithely with or without permission of any sort. He was merely relieved that this wretched interview had come to a close.

"But Damian—"

He froze halfway to the door. Of course it couldn't be that easy. Next his uncle would no doubt make him admit that he was beginning to harbor hopes for the future. He'd make him call it something utterly vile like a 'life plan' or some such nonsense.

"If I find out that you are doing this to get close to Miss Pottermouth—"

His short laugh of amusement cut Uncle Edward off before he could finish. Damian turned around. "I assure you, Uncle, I have no nefarious intentions toward the Dowager Demon's niece."

Uncle Edward scowled at the nickname but did not argue.

How could he? The dowager duchess's property had adjoined theirs since time immemorial and his uncle knew their neighbor's character as well as anyone.

Was it any wonder that her ward had been such an unpleasant little brat?

Likely not.

He felt his lips curling in disgust at this flicker of sympathy for the girl who'd made his childhood miserable with her relentless tattling and her ceaseless nagging.

Certainly, she'd been the victim of bad fortune to be raised by the Dowager Demon but that hardly excused her for being a prig.

Uncle Edward was watching him closely. "Are you certain you have no ulterior motives when it comes to Miss Pottermouth?"

Damian rolled his eyes. Did he really have to repeat himself? Couldn't his uncle have a little trust just this once? But as soon as Damian thought it, he dismissed the idea.

Of course his uncle didn't trust his word. Why should he? Aside from the fact that his uncle knew very well of his questionable parentage, he had a lifetime of bad behavior to live down.

Or to live up to, depending how one looked at it.

The thought made him grin.

Uncle Edward groaned as he ran a weary hand over his face. "That smile only ever leads to trouble."

Damian laughed, heading toward the door. "Perhaps. But I can promise you this." He paused in the doorway. "I have no nefarious hidden agendas when it comes to Miss Prudence Pottermouth."

Uncle Edward's eyes narrowed with suspicion. "So you don't have any..." He waved a hand, his expression pained. "Feelings for the girl."

Damian laughed again, because honestly, the thought was ludicrous. He knew what his uncle meant by 'feelings.' He meant attraction. Desire.

It had been years since he'd seen the girl but all he felt when he thought of Miss Prudence Pottermouth was contempt.

3

*P*rudence's great aunt wasted no time.

The very next morning, Prudence was summoned from the breakfast table—a table at which the servants had been ordered to provide only the bare minimum because of her 'weight troubles.'

How mortifying.

Her stomach still rumbled with hunger as she left the room at her aunt's bidding. "We have a full day ahead of us," her aunt said the moment she entered the drawing room.

Her aunt eyed her from head to toe and she straightened her spine in response, bracing herself for the inevitable criticisms.

Fortunately, this morning her aunt seemed too distracted to delve into specifics and she settled on a simple shake of her head. "We have much work to do."

Prudence held still. That was it?

She very nearly wilted with relief, but that would have meant that her posture worsened and that would have only incurred more criticism.

So she remained standing as straight as an arrow, her

back to the door as she listened to her aunt rattle off a list of all the steps they would take for her improvement.

They had a fortnight to prepare for her possible future husband's arrival with his family, and Aunt Eleanor meant to make the most of every last second.

"But most importantly, your music lessons." Aunt Eleanor's gaze turned sharp. "If you cannot master the pianoforte then perhaps he can teach you how to hold a tune so you don't embarrass yourself by singing."

The mere mention of singing had her throat closing up in horror.

"Or we'll find you some other instrument." Aunt Eleanor waved a hand as though there were a wide assortment of instruments to be found in the drawing room. "Something that you can't ruin with those thick fingers of yours."

Prudence nodded. All she had to do was try, she reminded herself. It was not as though this engagement would be made or broken based on her ability to sing, now would it?

Her aunt took a step closer as the door behind Prudence opened and the butler cleared his throat.

Her aunt took no notice. "Do you understand the gravity of this situation, Prudence?"

She nodded. "Of course."

"Of course," her aunt repeated with a scornful mutter. "I doubt it. If you did, you would have tried harder at Miss Grayson's school. But you didn't so now you are here, and do not think for one moment that I will coddle you or allow you to be the lazy ungrateful little cur your mother was as a child."

The words were barbed arrows, but years of practice taught her how to shield herself against their blows. "Yes, Aunt Eleanor."

But Aunt Eleanor wasn't done. "Do you think Mr. Benedict couldn't have his pick of ladies? Do you believe you are so very special that he will overlook such a monumental flaw?"

She ought to keep quiet. She knew this very well. Yet her entire body quaked with the urge to speak, to protest, to defend herself. "But I have many other skills—"

"*Other* skills?" Her aunt's face grew flushed and her entire body seemed to quiver with anger.

Fear sliced through Prudence, cold and sickening as she stumbled back a step.

"Do you think Mr. Benedict cares that you can do maths? Do you think he will be so very overcome by your *spectacular* looks that he'll forget the fact that he is in need of a wife who can host and that his very business depends on having a wife who can entertain?"

She was still trying to stammer a response when a voice from behind her saved her.

"My apologies for intruding, my lady."

That voice. She knew that voice.

Spinning around quickly, she found herself right smack in the middle of her worst nightmare.

Him.

Damian the reckless beast was there, in the doorway...and he'd heard.

He'd heard it all, of that she was certain. When his dark gaze flickered in her direction she saw it—worse than any tirade or criticism her aunt could ever throw her way.

Pity.

She saw pity there, and it was so much worse than her friends' sympathy. It made her insides recoil, her stomach churn.

It made her want to heave those meager contents in her stomach to rid herself of the vile sensation.

"You are late." Her aunt snapped at him as she strode

toward the door, past Prudence, who no longer seemed to exist. The tirade forgotten.

"Apologies again, my lady." Damian bowed low, his gaze cast down to the floor in respect.

Prudence narrowed her eyes, registering him anew now that the shock of his sudden arrival was waning.

"I arrived a short while ago but did not wish to intrude."

Her aunt glared at the butler who cowered beside him as he murmured an apology for not interrupting sooner, although Prudence was certain that they all knew he would have been chastised either way. The poor old servant was forever in trouble.

"Hmph." Her aunt gave a grunt that no one would refer to as ladylike as she eyed Damian from head to toe.

Prudence did the same from a safe distance.

What she found was remarkable. It was him…and it wasn't.

There was no denying those dark eyes, that sharp jawline, the narrow, aquiline nose, or those cheekbones that hinted at a heritage she could not quite place.

There was something beautifully exotic about him, with his thick, dark hair and his tall, lean build. He'd always stood apart from any crowd, and at this moment she would have recognized him anywhere, even if a few years of aging had given him a bit more of a mature look.

No, he *looked* exactly the same as she remembered. But his demeanor…

Well, this was new.

Gone was the roguish, disreputable rake with the languid air, the hooded eyes, and the ever present smirk. In his place was a dignified, upright, superior sort of man.

The kind of man her aunt adored. One who cast young ladies such as herself a derisive glance before turning their allegiance and respect to whomever held the most power.

In this case—in most cases—that meant her great aunt.

"I assure you, I will have your niece ready in time for her next performance," he was saying in that low voice of his. Although rather than that smug, sarcastic tone she'd always despised, his voice now was filled with reverence and respect.

"Be sure that you do," Aunt Eleanore snapped. "Your reputation precedes you, Lord Damian. But if you cannot deliver as promised, I shall be forced to let my friends know that your talents have been exaggerated."

He dipped his head low in acknowledgment, showing none of the fear that many would in his position, but none of that galling bravado either.

Prudence's eyes narrowed further. What was he about? Had he truly changed so very much? Had he matured into this man she saw before her or was this some sort of act?

Mistrust had her pinching her lips to keep from asking him outright, something she would certainly have done if her aunt were not here in the room with them.

His gaze flicked past Aunt Eleanor and clashed with hers, and that was when she saw it clear as day.

His mockery. His silent laughter at her expense.

Oh, nothing had changed in his outward demeanor, but she didn't need it to. She knew. She could see right through this act of his and the fact that her great aunt was fooled—and she surely was because even now she was walking out of the room and leaving them alone together, telling the butler to leave the door open and stay close, but otherwise leaving them alone.

Together.

Something she could not name had her heart racing in her chest. Or maybe it wasn't some*thing* but several things. She could not tell if what she was feeling was panic, fear, disgust, or anger.

She suspected it was all of the above.

His gaze held hers as her aunt threw out one last parting shot to Prudence about trying her best or not bothering to join her for supper.

Prudence flinched slightly but waited to breathe again until her aunt left the room and a sudden silence filled the air in her wake.

All she could hear was the sound of her own breathing in the muffled room with its thick carpeting and outdated, oversized furniture that used to make her feel like a human visiting a giant's kingdom when she was a child.

She couldn't recall ever seeing Damian in this room or in this house, despite their long acquaintance. Perhaps that was why she found it so unsettling. His presence here felt ominous...and that was *before* he opened his mouth.

"And so we meet again, Pru."

She frowned. "It's Miss Pottermouth."

He arched a brow and….there he was. Her breath caught in her throat and her eyes widened. The transformation was remarkable. As if a curtain was drawn back, she found herself facing the boy who'd terrorized her youth with his merciless teasing and his awful pranks.

"I've called you Pru for years," he said, his eyes dancing with mirth. "And now so formal?"

She pinched her lips together. He was baiting her. This time—for once—she wouldn't fall for it. "We were children then. Times have changed."

"Ah." He clapped a hand over his heart. "And here I'd hoped you'd call me Damian once more and we could rekindle our childhood intimacy."

She scowled. "We were never intimate."

He gave his head a woeful shake. "And more's the pity."

She opened her mouth. She closed her mouth. "What are you on about?" Planting her hands on her hips, she eyed him as he'd been studying her. "And what is with this music tutor nonsense? Surely your uncle doesn't approve—"

"I have my uncle's full support," he interrupted.

She narrowed her eyes. He seemed to be telling the truth.

But then again, unlike her, his guardian had always been kind and supportive. No doubt this was why he'd also been so disobedient as a child.

As though he could read her thoughts, his eyes narrowed and his lips twitched with a mocking smirk. "What's wrong, Pru? Worried I'll cause you trouble?"

"I would not put it past you."

He laughed. "You can rest assured, my days of hijinx and pranks are well behind me."

"I see. Now you merely act the part of the proper young gentleman while you weasel your way into the private rooms of the *ton*'s most eligible young ladies."

His brows shot up in surprise and the flickering look in his eyes was a mix of irritation and admiration—which precisely summed up the way he'd always treated her. Even as a child he could not seem to determine whether she was a worthy adversary or merely a pest.

He recovered quickly, a sinister smile replacing his smirk as he strode toward her, not stopping until he was so close she could feel his heat. "Is that what worries you, Pru?" He glanced down, taking in her modest, perhaps slightly frumpy morning gown, and moving up to eye her tidy but practical hairstyle. "I assure you, you have nothing to fear on that front."

She pursed her lips, narrowed her eyes...but a dreadful heat rose up in her neck, no doubt leaving her decolletage a mottled, ugly sight as his meaning registered.

She had nothing to fear because she was not attractive enough to warrant his attentions.

Tilting her chin up higher, she sniffed. "Good. I'm glad we are clear."

His dark eyes flashed, and for a moment she was nearly knocked sideways because something passed between them. An understanding, perhaps. The wicked banter and the unpleasant insinuations fell away and for a moment it was just Pru and Damian.

And in that moment, in his eyes, she caught something alarmingly like guilt. Maybe regret. There and gone so fast she nearly missed it.

"Are you ready then, *Miss Pottermouth*?" He said her name mockingly.

She wasn't entirely sure what prompted her to do it, but she shot back with, "After you, Damian."

His eyes flared wide with surprise and amusement before he led them toward the music room. For a moment, her dislike for Damian was forgotten. It was drowned out by dread.

That dread grew to panic as they entered the large, wood-paneled room with its oriental rug and the ferns that added little life to the stale, memory-filled room.

He turned as he reached the pianoforte. "Now then, Miss Pottermouth, where shall we beg—" He stopped abruptly as he faced her. "Pru?"

His brows drew down in an expression she'd never seen from him before—and she'd thought she'd catalogued his every smirk, smile, and sneer.

But this didn't fall into any of those categories. This was a frown. And frowns made him look different. They made him seem more mature, more serious.

And that look in his eyes?

Was that…?

She couldn't be certain.

And then it didn't matter because the room was spinning.

That panicky sensation giving way to a sick feeling that was enhanced a million times over by the familiar scent of this room, with its wood polish and that musty stench from the curtains.

"Miss Potter—oh curse it. Pru, are you all right?"

The room ceased spinning just long enough for her to catch sight of the concern in his eyes.

Concern. Now that was definitely a new look from this man.

That was the last thought she had before she lost all sight and the room went dark.

4

Damian's heart stopped when Prudence collapsed.

Instinct had him rushing over to her and catching her just before her head made contact with the floor. But now he was stuck holding her in an awkward grip, half crouching and half kneeling as he attempted to gently lower her weight.

He might not like Prudence but he had no wish to see her harmed.

In fact, the sight of her lying prostrate like this, all vulnerable and fragile and—

Pfft. He let out a little scoff of rueful amusement. Fragile? Prudence? Hardly. The girl was a force of nature.

And yet...

He tapped her cheek gently, her head lolling in his lap as he adjusted to make her comfortable. Should he call for assistance?

Most likely.

He stared down at her features, so sweet when they weren't pinched in distaste or pursed with judgement. So surprisingly...pretty.

He frowned down at her as he felt for her pulse at her neck. Steady. Her chest was rising and falling normally.

He was no doctor but she seemed to have merely fainted. And truth be told, the last thing he wanted was another run-in with her great aunt. More importantly, he had no desire to give the Dowager Demon another reason to criticize poor Pru.

Poor Pru. He exhaled loudly in exasperation. He'd never felt sorry for this girl before and he wasn't keen on the feeling. More, he had a suspicion that she would hate it if she knew he was pitying her.

But he couldn't quite shake the sight of her when she'd been bearing the brunt of her aunt's harsh words. Even from behind he could see it, the way her normally rigid posture seemed to slump beneath her aunt's criticisms. And when she'd turned, he'd seen it in her eyes. The sort of weary resignation he'd never thought to see in someone so rigidly sure of herself and the world around her.

"Come on, Pru, wake up." He shook her shoulder gently. "Wake up for me, Prudence."

Her eyes fluttered open, her long lashes a dark sweep against her pale cheek.

She *was* rather pretty. Which was disturbing. At what point had priggish Prudence Pottermouth become pretty?

He frowned. He wasn't sure he liked this change in her. She'd always been plain. A bit on the plump side, with forgettable features and frumpy clothes.

He eyed her now. All peaceful like this, he could see her with new eyes. Those features were exactly the same, but without a scowl, they weren't plain at all.

And she was still not slim, but how had he ever found her to be plump? She was curvaceous. Luscious, even.

He tore his gaze away, back to her face.

But the clothes...those were still frumpy. If she wore something fitted, she might actually be appealing.

He felt a smirk forming as he eyed her lips, which had a perfect cupid's bow when she wasn't frowning.

He imagined how she'd respond if he told her that she was appealing to members of the opposite sex. She'd slap him for his impertinence, no doubt.

Her eyes shot open and he was caught grinning down at her.

She blinked, her pupils dilating as her gaze focused on him. With lightning fast movements, her eyes flickered to the left and right, up and down, taking in him and her surroundings.

He saw the moment her current position became clear to her.

"Oh! What am I...why am I...?" She didn't bother to answer before rolling sideways off his lap, landing on all fours with all the grace and charm of a feral cat.

"Feeling better, I see." He brushed off his pants and came to stand, reaching a hand down to help her up. She ignored it.

"What did I...?" She cut herself off and her cheeks turned a fetching shade of pink. "Oh dear."

He tilted his head to the side. "Do you often faint, Miss Pottermouth? Or was it my company that made you swoon?"

Her lips pinched together and he just barely held back a laugh. She was just too easy to tease.

And besides, he'd discovered only today that he far preferred an irritated Pru to a pitiable one, and he suspected she felt the same.

Her gaze dropped but her chin went up as she stiffened her spine and clasped her hands together before her. "I apologize."

He gave a snort of amusement. "Apologize? You?"

Her gaze flicked up to meet his as her brows drew down. "A proper gentleman would ease my discomfort and pretend this never happened."

"Yes, well, this gentleman thinks an apology is ridiculous. It wasn't as though you intended to fall at my feet." He found far too much enjoyment in the way her blush spread. "Or did you?"

She blinked in surprise, her brows arching. "Pardon me?"

"Admit it." He took a few steps toward her, feeling more alert and alive than he had in...oh, ages. Funny, he'd always despised this girl but he'd forgotten how diverting it could be to tease her. "You were looking for a way to wind up in my arms."

She smacked his arm so quickly it made his head jerk back, with such force that he found himself cradling his left bicep. "Was that really necessary?"

"Yes." She tilted her chin up with such dignity, one would never imagine that she'd been strewn across his lap, limp as a rag doll not two minutes prior. "How else will you learn to behave?" She added a sniff for good measure.

He stared at her, torn between a laugh and a shout of exasperation. What came out was a choking sound that had her frowning at him anew.

"Why are you so amused?" she asked, her tone wary.

He shook his head, shaking off his surprise in the process. "Merely shocked to find that you are in favor of corporal punishment." He leaned in and lowered his voice. "I will keep that in mind during our lessons."

She blinked and a second later she jerked back as if just now realizing how close they were standing.

Close enough that he could see how pale she was and the shadows beneath her eyes. His eyes narrowed on her. "Are you well?" He frowned. "Have you been eating?"

Her lips curved into a sneer. "Is that supposed to be a

joke?"

His brows drew together in confusion. "Pardon?"

"Nevermind." She looked away and then turned back, suspicion replacing whatever emotion had been there. Something he couldn't quite place. Something that seemed almost like embarrassment, but that couldn't be right.

"You have not changed at all, have you?" She didn't seem to expect an answer. Her gaze slid over him with the sort of judgement that always made him bristle.

It was a look that said he'd been catalogued, weighed, assessed, and found wanting. She'd always looked at him thus, ever since his uncle had taken him in. As though she could see right past his uncle's title he was set to inherit and straight through to his less than perfect bloodline.

Oh, he'd been born on the right side of the blanket, but that was about the only thing his parents had done right. His father had married for love, not caring a whit that his wife was of gypsy blood and that by marrying her and bearing a child they would be forever on the outside of society.

Not caring, that is, until he was forced to live as an outsider, with all the whispers and scandal that came with it. And while his uncle had done his best to put the gossip to rest after the unfortunate carriage accident that left him an orphan, there were some who would always judge.

Prudence was one of them. He wasn't even certain she knew anything about his parents, but she found him lacking all the same. Always had and always would.

He leaned back against the pianoforte and crossed his arms, letting himself relax. He despised her sneers and her judgment, but there was something rather freeing about being seen for what one was.

There were no pretenses to be maintained around this girl...for better or for worse.

"How did you do it?" she demanded.

He arched his brows with a smirk that he knew would drive her to distraction.

Good.

"How did I do what?"

She narrowed her eyes further, suspicion morphing into accusation. "How did you delude my aunt and all the other ladies of the *ton* into believing that you are some sort of…" She waved a hand in irritation. "Musical genius."

One corner of his mouth hitched up at that. "Musical genius, eh? Is that what they are calling me?"

Her answer was to purse her lips.

"What else do they call me?" He arched his brows playfully, loving the way her nostrils flared as she fought the urge to shout at him. Or perhaps strike him again.

She cocked her head to the side. "You've somehow managed to convince my aunt that you are some well-disciplined tutor." She squinted. "How?"

"I'm afraid I don't understand the question," he lied. "I am quite skilled when it comes to music and I have worked veritable miracles amongst the *ton*'s leading ladies—"

"But you are still an impossible rogue," she snapped.

He shrugged. What was the point in denying it? "Perhaps, but I have gotten much better at playing whatever role benefits me."

Her expression was an odd one. He couldn't quite tell if she was pleased to have been proven correct or had just taken a bite of something particularly sour.

"What about the role of a dutiful young lord, an heir to a marquess?"

He shook his head, attempting to keep his expression unmoved. "That will never happen. My uncle is still young enough to remarry, and he ought to sire a son of his own."

Her gaze was shockingly even. Absurdly intense. She would not let this go.

Sure enough... "Do you mean to tell me that you do not wish to be heir? How does your uncle feel about the matter?"

He let out an exasperated sigh. "I do not see why you should concern yourself with my future or my relationship to my uncle or the title."

She continued to stare. She didn't look away until he gestured toward the instrument behind him, shifting to make way for her. "Shall we get started or do you plan to faint again?"

She let out a *harrumph* sound that had him hiding a grin but when he glanced back he found her hesitating. "Pru?"

"It's Miss Pottermouth." But her protest lacked the heat it ought to have.

He arched a brow, waiting her out. This wasn't the first young woman who was intimidated at the thought of performing for him...the musical genius.

The thought made him smirk as he waited for her to overcome her nerves.

He ought to have known better. Pru was not one to submit, not without a fight.

"This is highly improper," she said, crossing her arms in defiance. "You are a marquess's nephew, you should not be tutoring young ladies."

"Why are you so caught up on my potential title?" He hated the fact that she'd caused his cool demeanor to slip, but he hated it even more that she would not cease reminding him of the duties and obligations that he dreaded. He took a deep breath. "I told you I neither want it, nor plan on it—"

"Yes, but—"

"What is your real problem here?" he demanded.

"You are not fit to be a tutor."

He blinked once. Twice. "Excuse me?"

Her nostrils flared with her inhale, the only sign that she was flustered. Not angry, he thought. Just...nervous. On edge.

How odd.

"This is beneath you," she continued.

Now he was actually growing concerned. "You think that this is beneath me?"

"Of course it is," she huffed. "Tutoring young ladies? Getting paid for it? It's...unseemly."

"How kind of you to worry about my reputation."

She rolled her eyes at his dry tone. "I'm not worried about you."

He could practically see her scrambling for an excuse. "I'm worried about your uncle's good opinion, that is all. Surely he cannot approve of this new business you've gone into—"

"On the contrary. He's relieved to find that I have some ambition, after all. This all started because he cut me off, you know—"

"No!" Her gaping stare was nicely shocked.

"Yes. He and all the other upright morally superior stuffed-shirts of the ton have decided that my new pastime is one to be commended." He made a show of rolling his hand as he bowed low. "A youthful rake making amends for his past misdeeds...at your service."

He heard a choking sound. A scoff, no doubt. He looked up, ready to find a sneer on her face.

He felt as though he'd been smacked upside the head to discover a genuine smile instead. It faded quickly as she looked away but for a moment there...for just a second he'd thought...

Had he made her *laugh*?

The surge of triumph was bizarre and completely out of proportion to the situation. And yet, he couldn't deny the heady pleasure of having once—*finally*—made priggish Pru laugh.

"So you've managed to convince your uncle that you have

reformed then?" she asked.

He shrugged. If this was anyone else talking he would have lied. He would have spun a tale about how he had indeed seen the errors of his ways after his years of carousing with other young gentlemen of the *ton*, spending too much money for the pleasure of drinking and dining and gambling.

But truth be told, he did not regret those activities. Nor did he feel wrong for being a man of leisure. It was merely that he'd grown bored with it, that was all. "My uncle is hardly suffering some mistaken assumption about my basic character."

"And what is that, exactly?" She rested a hand on her waist and jutted a hip out to the side. He knew she was not trying to appear enticing...but she still succeeded.

He looked away quickly, temporarily stunned into stupidity over the thought that he had just been ogling Prudence Pottermouth, the world's least appealing female.

He glanced back. Or, at least, she had been. At what point had that changed?

She was waiting for an answer and he shook off all thoughts of distraction. What was his true character? Well, she ought to know better than anyone. "Why, I'm a knave, of course."

He gave her his best wicked grin and got a sneer in response.

This was more like it. Enemies to the end. Her sneers were far more familiar and put him back on even footing.

"If you're still such a scoundrel then why did you agree to help me?"

"For the money, of course. My uncle cut me off last year, and I've been paying my own way ever since."

She blinked in surprise. "Really?"

He nodded.

"Good for him."

A shocked laugh escaped before he could stop it. "Yes, well, now that you understand my motives and I yours—"

"What do you know of my motives?" Her eyes were narrowed with suspicion again.

He moved toward her slowly. "Tell me, did something happen to you as a child to make you so suspicious all the time?"

She sniffed. "Yes. I was forced to be playmates with a heathenous neighbor who lived to torture me."

He started to laugh which made her eyes narrow even further.

"I developed the good sense to be wary whenever he seemed too pleased with himself." She arched one brow. "His pleasure could only ever mean my doom."

"Your doom!" he crowed. "Oh, I like that. A frog in your bedding could hardly be considered your *doom*."

Her lips twitched and he could practically see her cataloguing his every indiscretion, ready to hurl them at him as she always did. She couldn't bear to let an occasion pass when she could throw his bad deeds in his face.

But that was the past, and this was his present, and his future…

He gave his head a sharp shake. He had no desire to think of the future. He had a mission to complete and while willful and obstinate, he was certain he could help Miss Prudence Pottermouth.

"Your motives," he said, bringing them back to the topic at hand. "That seems easy enough to suss out, even for one such as me." He eyed her from head to toe, trying not to grin when her blush spread.

Blushing was new.

He liked it. It meant that while she might treat him as the boy he once was, she saw him as the man he'd become.

"You wish to marry," he said softly. "And you are expected to marry well."

She sniffed.

"Is it still that Benedict chap you're set to marry?"

She pursed her lips.

His mind was racing back to the bits and pieces of gossip he'd picked up over the years. There was an understanding between the families and to be honest, he'd been surprised to find that she returned to the Dowager Demon's house unmarried. He hadn't given her much thought since she'd been shipped off to that finishing school years ago, but if he had he would have guessed that she'd been happily married by now.

Well, not *happily*.

Pru never did anything happily.

"I thought that agreement was as good as done—"

"Yes, well, apparently not." Her voice was clipped, her lips curved up in that sneer he despised. And yet...

There was a flicker of uncertainty there that made it impossible to come back at her with a barb about how she had likely driven off the poor man.

Her gaze flickered away from his. "Aunt Eleanor fears I'm not quite...satisfactory." Her throat worked as she swallowed and he wondered how much it pained Miss Perfect Pru to admit it.

"So music is your fatal flaw, I assume." He tried for teasing but was horrified to find that his tone fell just shy of sympathetic.

That would not do. Neither of them wished for his pity.

She nodded. "You assume correctly."

He rocked back on his feet. After years of hating Pru's smugness and her superior attitude, he was horrified to find that he liked this humble side of her even less.

She looked...shorter. She seemed to be shrinking right in

front of his eyes. He tilted his head to the side. Had she always been so small?

Funny, he'd always seen her as a formidable enemy. A sword-wielding virago from Greek mythology. Of course she wielded sharp words in lieu of a sword, but even so, the image had stuck in his mind and finding out now that she was—well, *human*...

It was upsetting.

Her gaze flicked up to meet his and she stiffened. "Stop looking at me like that."

"Like what?"

"As though you feel sorry for me."

He scoffed. "Trust me, Pru, you are the last person I'd feel sorry for."

"Good." She straightened and he had a flash of the warrior, and the world righted itself nicely. She glanced toward the pianoforte with the sort of set chin and straight shoulders one would expect from a soldier going into battle. "I will master this topic, and once I do I will prove to my aunt and to...to everyone that I can be the perfect wife."

"Perfect," he repeated. Ought he to tell her that no one is perfect? He eyed her closely. It seemed cruel to burst her newfound hope. "Of course you will."

She shot him a quick look. Suspicion again. She feared he was mocking her...and he was. But only a little.

He moved to stand beside her so they were both facing the instrument. "You will master music, Pru." He grinned. "I will make sure of it."

Her expression wavered between wariness and hope. "Truly?"

He leaned down, catching a whiff of a floral scent that was soft and sweet and beguilingly feminine—and totally at odds with every other hard edge of her personality. "I promise."

5

*S*he shouldn't have been surprised that a man like Damian was making promises he couldn't keep.

What was more shocking was that he seemed to be unaware that he would fail. "Right." He lifted a fist to his mouth, his expression uncharacteristically grim as he eyed her hands on the keys as though they were a riddle he could not quite solve.

She just barely held back a sigh. After all, for three days straight now he had made good on his promise.

Or at least, he'd tried.

He'd tried harder than she would have thought he was capable of trying. For a gentleman who'd made a name for himself as a lazy ne'er-do-well, he was shockingly devoted to this cause.

She grimaced as she followed his gaze to her fingers, which *were* rather stumpy as her aunt had helpfully pointed out over supper the night before.

She moved her hands from his critical gaze now, wiping them on her skirts. As always, the moment she lifted her hands to play, the metronome ticking away above her head and her new tutor hovering behind her, her silly palms grew clammy. Her fingers felt frozen. And her heart…

Well, her heart seemed to be in competition with the metronome, racing faster and faster until it left that relentless even ticking in the dust.

"This is not working." His words were gruff and quiet, but they struck her like a bolt of lightning.

She jumped out of her seat, panic rising up her throat. "Please do not give up on me."

His eyes widened but she'd known this moment was coming—it always came eventually. Even Miss Grayson's kind old music instructor had patted her hand gently and told her she was a lost cause.

Not in so many words, of course, but the meaning was the same.

"Pru, we cannot—"

"Please." She clasped her clammy hands together pleadingly. Her pride raged. Her sense of fairness rebelled. But she'd been bracing herself for this moment for the last few days and had promised herself that she would not let him go without a fight.

For, whether she wished to admit it or not, she needed his help.

Badly.

It might be in vain, but she had to at least try not to humiliate herself in front of her aunt and her would-be husband. If her aunt was correct, and entertaining was so vitally important to Mr. Benedict then she needed to be up to snuff.

Or at least passable.

At this point, she would settle for passable.

"I assure you, I have been working diligently on the exercises you gave me," she started, the words coming a bit easier now that her pride was well and truly trampled beneath her feet. She'd rehearsed what she'd say when the time came when Damian decided she was beyond saving and threatened to quit. "I have been working every minute of the day and—"

"That is precisely the problem."

She blinked up at him. "Er...pardon?"

He pressed his lips together, his nostrils flaring with irritation. "I said, that is your problem."

"My problem? But you told me to practice and everyone knows that practice makes perfect."

"Who told you that lie?"

She was only moderately relieved to see that his irritation was giving way to his usual amusement. Even if it was at her expense, she preferred this teasing, mocking Damian. When he was serious—or worse, sympathetic—she knew not what to make of him.

"First of all," he continued, his arms crossed as he looked down his nose at her. "Perfection does not exist in the world of music." He lifted a hand to jab a finger in her direction. "That is your second problem."

Her brows came up. "I have two problems now?"

His sigh was exaggerated. "Pru, you have more problems than I can count, but for now, I am merely concerned with the problems that are making this—" He jabbed a finger toward the pianoforte, "sound like an instrument of torture."

"I-why that-I never..." Her blustery protests trailed off meekly as her gaze once more fell on the dreaded keys. It *had* sounded rather like something was being tormented.

Probably the composer's soul.

Her lips twitched upward at her own self-deprecating joke. Gallows humor at its finest because her failure to master an instrument could very well mean the death of her future.

She scowled down at her fingers at that thought.

Surely not. Of course her aunt said as much, but her aunt

was nothing if not extreme. If Prudence had failed to master embroidery then she supposed embellished handkerchiefs would be the defining factor in Mr. Benedict's quest for a wife.

No, her aunt expected perfection—she demanded it. And Prudence had always done her best to deliver, but in this regard...

She sighed as her hands rested on the keys, making a discordant sound that was somehow superior to her entire performance. "I suppose you're right. I am hopeless."

"Who said that?" The anger in his voice had her looking up. He crossed his arms again. "Who on earth told you that you were hopeless?"

"Well, you said that I had—"

"You have problems, yes. Obviously." He frowned and shook his head. "Really, Pru, were you always prone to such melodrama?"

She bit her lip as she studied him. "So you are not quitting then?"

His brows arched up high, his eyes widening in shock or horror, or perhaps both. "Quitting? Me? Never." One corner of his mouth hitched up in a lopsided little smile that was at once familiar and utterly new.

Or at least, the sensation it brought about in her was entirely new.

"You have it all wrong, Pru. I'm not about to quit." He headed toward the glass doors leading to the garden. "Not when I've only just begun."

She hurried after him, glancing back anxiously at the still-open doors. It was one thing to be playing music alone with the door open and servants forever hurrying in and out to keep an eye on them. But now he was leading her away from the house, into the thicket of trees.

"Where are you taking me?"

"Away."

"Away from what?" She quickened her steps to catch up to him. "Away from good sense, perhaps? It's freezing out here."

"Tomorrow I shall remember to bring you a cloak, but for today we don't have much time and not a minute to waste."

"For what?" Her breathing was growing ragged and she hated that he wasn't even slightly out of breath when he smiled down at her.

"For the real learning to begin."

His grin was utterly wicked as he strode ahead until they were out of sight of the main house.

"For the real learning to begin," she muttered under her breath. How on earth did he manage to make that sound so ominous?

They reached a clearing and he stopped so suddenly she ran smack into his back. He whipped around and caught her as she stumbled back, keeping her from falling on her backside, not that one more humiliation mattered at this point.

The man she'd despised since she was a child was a first-hand witness to her worst failure...what was another fall at his feet?

Despair threatened and she swallowed it down with a frown. "What are you about, Damian?"

He smirked at her use of his given name. After countless prods and teasing she'd finally caved to the improper use of their given names and it seemed to bring him no end of joy.

He didn't drop his grip from her arms, not even when she tugged. He made a tsking sound, that was part chiding, part soothing—the sort of sound she suspected he made when his horse was scared during a storm.

She frowned at the thought. "Why are you shushing me?"

"I merely want you to relax." He tugged her closer, wrapping an arm about her waist.

She pulled her upper body away as far as his embrace

would allow, her heart surging up into her throat at this intimate contact. He was so close his scent enveloped her and his body seemed to swallow her whole. "I would be far more relaxed if you were to release me," she said as she pushed against his chest.

He narrowed his eyes. "Calm yourself, Pru, you have my word that I am not attempting to take liberties."

"Then what are you—oh!" His free hand grabbed hers and held it up. And all at once they were waltzing.

Or he was attempting to, at least. He was moving in time to some tune she could not hear and she was stumbling along with him because...where else could she go?

Like a rag doll in his arms, she flailed wildly until he stopped with a sigh. "Listen, Pru. That is all you are required to do for this portion of your lesson."

She stared up at him in the silence that was this thicket of trees. He had lost his mind. No doubt too many spirits over the years. Too much revelry had led this formerly sane yet wicked rogue to lose his sanity.

It was a shame, really. Particularly since he was holding her in his arms.

His eyes were lit with something she couldn't explain. Fanaticism, perhaps, or maybe just passion. Whatever it was, it felt foreign to her. She'd never been one for passion, just logic.

"Are you listening, Pru?" he asked, his voice hushed. Reverent.

"Listening? To what?"

He started to move again, and this time she managed to keep pace, but just barely. "The music, Pru, listen for the music."

She blinked dazedly. Music? Listening? What was he on about? He was teasing her. She ought to be angry.

She definitely should not feel like swooning again. She'd

eaten breakfast this morning, there was absolutely no reason for her to feel dizzy.

"Close your eyes," he ordered.

Her eyelids fluttered a few times but she fought the urge to obey his command. What was wrong with her?

"Just close them, Pru." It was his little smile of understanding that convinced her to finally relent and shut her eyes.

His smile seemed to say 'I know you think I'm a lunatic, but I promise I have my reasons.'

When she'd started to be able to read so much into a smile, she didn't know.

"Trust me," he whispered near her ear.

She frowned because...she did. To a certain extent, at least. Her body might have felt lit from within at the intimate touch, and his scent and his voice were doing odd things to her head, but she was not afraid.

And she supposed any normal lady would be.

But then again, he knew better than most that she was not normal. Nor was she fun or passionate or witty or anything else that would appeal to a wicked man like Damian.

"Do you hear it now?" he asked.

She huffed, ignoring the buzz she felt throughout her body when he talked so close to her ear like that. "Hear what?" She strained her ears. Did he truly hear something or was he playing tricks on her again?

She remembered the servants talking this morning. A fair was coming to town a few days hence. The center of town was miles away but she supposed it was possible that his sensitive ears could pick up on some performers rehearsing.

She furrowed her brow and concentrated but all she could hear was the whistle of wind in the trees overhead and the grass whispering beneath their feet. If she listened very closely she could even hear her own pulse.

Her hand in his was guided between them. Resting her hand on his chest his fingers covered hers and began to pat hers in time to a beat.

To her beat.

To their beat.

She blinked her eyes open in surprise. He was beating a tune in time with their heartbeats. The little smile he wore held no taunting and no mockery.

It was almost...sweet. Gentle. "Do you feel that?" he asked. "That is rhythm."

She nodded slowly, her steps matching his as she felt the beat, on her hand and in her chest. Concentrating on the feel of it so much so that it seemed to swell around her, to fill the air between them.

"Close your eyes." This time his command was a whisper and she didn't hesitate. "Now do you hear it?"

Confusion and frustration had her brows drawing down, her lips pursing. "Hear what? All I hear is the wind and the grass."

"Precisely." His voice was so low, as though he didn't want to disturb this so-called music.

Her eyes popped open. "It's not music, just background noise."

His lips twitched upward and as he spun her into a new dance step she did as he asked. For countless moments they spun and whirled and danced in time with the rhythm he'd set out and just when she was ready to throw her hands up and quit, she caught it.

A hint of a melody that seemed to be playing in time with their dancing. It was the wind. It was the grass. It was that combined with the sound of her skirts rustling and his breathing and the soft tap of his fingers on her hand.

She held her breath lest she lose it, but as she screwed her eyes shut he made that tsking sound again, pulling her in closer until she was resting against his body.

So very improper and yet she felt like he was telling her something without words. *Relax*, his body seemed to say. *Be easy*, his arms told her.

And so she loosened the tight furrowed brow and let her pinched lips part. She let herself relax into the sounds that swirled about them, creating a sort of melody of their own, and the rhythm that was pulsing so strongly now it was a wonder she'd never noticed it before.

"Music is always around you," he said, his voice blending into the moment rather than calling her out of it. With his low tone and the rumble of his chest, his voice was another note in the web that seemed to be surrounding her, hypnotizing her.

"It's around you, it's everywhere..." His voice was little more than a whisper. "It's inside you, even now. Do you feel it?"

Her yes came out on a breath that was little more than a sigh. Her body felt light and for the first time in her life, dancing didn't feel like a tedious chore but like something out of a dream. Effortless and weightless and....delightful.

Her eyelids fluttered open and reality returned all at once.

His eyes were right there, his nose was nearly brushing hers. His lips were...

She drew back with a gasp.

His lips were so close they'd nearly been kissing.

The moment she broke out of his embrace, the music stopped. The rhythm was ruined by her galloping heartbeat that drowned out all else.

He took a step toward her. "Pru..." Again with that tone like he was speaking to a spooked horse.

She glared at him. That tone was insulting.

He sighed and stopped moving toward her. "We'll continue tomorrow then, shall we?"

He didn't wait for an answer, and she didn't give one. She was too busy hurrying back to the house before her aunt discovered that she was missing.

6

Damian's uncle gave him the sort of disapproving look he was well used to, and it so closely resembled Pru's permanent expression that it gave him pause.

"Must you leave again?" his uncle demanded. The solicitor and the estate manager were already waiting in his uncle's office, waiting to discuss his uncle's holdings. "When you inherit one day—"

"If I inherit," he corrected, as he always did.

His uncle pinched the bridge of his nose and shut his eyes. Damian found himself thinking of Pru and the way she'd looked with her eyes shut. Every part of her being straining to hear music.

When she'd heard it...

His lungs hitched even now at the memory of her expression. Of the delight that had transformed her features and made her come alive in his arms.

That was the magic of music, he'd wished to say. But it was early days yet, and he and Pru had much work ahead of them.

He edged toward the front door. "Miss Pottermouth is

waiting, I'm afraid."

His uncle frowned. "So, you are still teaching her, then?"

"Of course. I made a commitment."

His uncle's face was a picture of a man torn. Damian could understand why. For nearly a decade, ever since he'd arrived on his uncle's doorstep, his good, kind, formidable uncle had been trying to teach him the meaning of commitment and hard work and responsibility etcetera, etcetera.

But in all those countless lectures, he'd likely never intended for Damian's sense of obligation to be used like this. Even though he was the son of a younger brother and one cast out of society, at that, his uncle still held hopes that he would be the heir of his dreams.

But Damian had no such hopes, and in some regards he thought he knew his uncle better than he knew himself.

The marquess had not given up on life and love quite as thoroughly as he might pretend.

His uncle just needed to realize that.

He slipped out the door before his uncle could figure out a way to argue that while making a commitment to teach a young lady was nice and all, it was not as important as taking the reins of his uncle's estate.

Learning to be a proper young lord was nearly as important to him as learning to be the perfect wife was to Prudence.

He made a sort of growling noise that made his horse whinny and shy away from him when he went to ride. "Sorry, Bert," he muttered to the old stallion he'd had since he was a teenager.

He couldn't stop brooding on the ride over, however. Between her great aunt's aggressive, cruel remarks even in front of him, or the way she'd all but pleaded with him to help her, Prudence was rapidly becoming a concern.

He was worried about her, and he'd never worried about

anyone before. Not since his parents died, at least. Once they'd left him he didn't have to fear what people said because it wouldn't get back to his mother and he wouldn't have to see her pain.

But now...

Well, now he felt that concern again. Even now, riding over on a beautiful cloudless day, all he could think about was what sort of hurtful comments her aunt might have made today.

Something about her weight, no doubt. He gripped the reins tighter as anger made his heart pound furiously. He'd overheard her the day before. And the day before that.

The Dowager Demon seemed to have little care for who heard her cruel and thoughtless remarks.

Her *inaccurate* remarks. Yesterday morning when he'd arrived, he'd overheard her telling Prudence that no gentleman worth his salt would want a cow for a wife.

If her aunt thought that any man would be turned off by the sight of curves in all the places women ought to have curves, then the old woman didn't know the first thing about the male species.

He groaned as memories came back to him—the very memories he'd been doing his best to forget ever since she'd walked away from three days before.

The feel of her in his arms. The way she'd melted into him, trusting him, relying on him, letting him lead. Her trust in him had been the first thing to tug at his heart.

Then it was the sight of her, concentrating so fiercely. The little warrior in his arms. But it was the delight when she'd heard it that he knew he'd remember until the day he died.

The look of sheer pleasure. Complete joy. It was a look he hadn't been aware she was capable of, but now that he'd seen it, he wanted to see it again, and again, and again.

He wanted that joy to be her norm, not the suspicion and wariness with which she seemed to regard the world.

His mind flashed back to the aunt's harsh words and he winced.

He supposed it was no wonder she viewed the world with such distrust if that cruel, bitter woman's voice was forever in her ear.

Even as he thought it, he heard her. Or rather he heard shouting as he handed over his reins to a stable boy and approached the house. The butler showed him into the music room and he could feel the havoc that Pru's aunt had wreaked.

She was nowhere to be seen, except for in the trembling of Prudence's lower lip.

"Ready for another lesson?" He tried to keep his voice calm, pleasant. He knew very well that his pity would only be met with contempt.

She was proud, his Pru. Always had been. Always would be. It was what made her such a fierce warrior.

She nodded, her head bowed over the piano, her fingers already going into position.

That was when he saw it. The red mark across her fingers. The painful welt that was forming and the way her head was bent so low as if…

"Pru?"

Her head came up slowly and he caught it. The shimmer of tears in her eyes before she blinked them away with an upward tilt of her chin.

His chest did something unwelcome. It seemed to tighten and twist all at once, his heart lurching at her pain and aching at the sight of her pride which wouldn't let her show it.

This girl was brave and strong…and more stubborn than a mule.

"Let's go," he snapped, his voice harsher than intended.

"Where to?" she asked.

"Anywhere but here." He wasn't even entirely sure where he was taking them when he sent word that they would need an escort.

"If Aunt Eleanor finds out—"

"Let her try and stop us." His growl had her eyes widening in surprise and it was with effort that he softened his tone and forced a smile. "I will deal with your aunt if she has an issue with our outing."

She arched one brow in doubt. His smile felt far more genuine at her look of disbelief. A flicker of the Pru he knew and—well, not *loved*. It was a flicker of the Prudence he knew and tolerated.

Still, it was good to see her again. For a moment there he'd thought he'd lost her.

"Come," he said when a footman announced that the carriage had been brought round.

"Where are we going?" she asked again when they reached the carriage and he helped her into her seat beside her lady's maid.

He had no idea but the sound of church bells in the distance gave him an idea. "We're heading into town." He turned to let the driver know and when he climbed in to join the ladies, he caught her frown.

"But there is a festival going on," she said.

He laughed at her confusion. "And so there is. The fall festival. You used to love it as a child."

Her frown intensified. "I did not. *You* loved it."

"Mmm." He nodded in agreement. "So I did. You should have loved it, though, and perhaps today I could show you why."

She huffed. "How is this supposed to help me improve in the music room?"

He tapped a finger to his temple. "I have my ways. Musical genius, remember?"

She rolled her eyes at the now-familiar joke, but he caught the twitch of her lips as she fought a grin. "I should never have told you that."

"Ah, but you did," he said, leaning back in his seat. "And now it is an absolute truth."

"Why?"

"Because the *ton* said so." He half turned to face her. "You've told me time and again that what society says is as good as law. It's akin to holy scripture, even, by your accounts."

She tsked, her gaze darting toward the lady's maid who was studiously ignoring them both. "Don't be sacrilegious."

"I am merely quoting you," he teased.

"And yet, I never said that." Her tone was all huffy and indignant, her lips pursed as usual, but there was no denying the laughter in her eyes. For a moment her gaze met his and held. For the first time in a long time—perhaps for the first time ever—they seemed to be in on the joke together. Not him mocking her, or her chiding him, but both of them finding humor in their own foibles.

He was incorrigible; she was a prig. And for once, that was rather amusing.

She looked away first. "I still do not see how this outing will improve my performance."

"Don't you?" He smiled when she gave the view outside her window the prickly glare he was so familiar with.

"There are no instruments at the fair," she pointed out as the bumpy dirt road they traveled upon grew cluttered with crowds heading toward town.

"Aren't there?" He pretended to be shocked and outright laughed when she turned that glare his way.

"So then how shall we practice?"

When he didn't immediately answer, her eyes clouded with something he could not name but hated more than life itself. "What shall I tell Aunt Eleanor when she asks?"

A muscle in his jaw twitched with anger.

Fear. That look he'd seen there in her eyes was fear...and he hated it. He'd loathe seeing that fear in anyone, but from Prudence—who might have been a goody-two-shoes, but was braver and more confident than most people he knew...

It was unbearable.

It made him want to shake some sense into her aunt, or at the very least steal Prudence away so she wouldn't have to face her again.

"Leave your aunt to me," was all he managed to say.

Something in his tone had her eyes widening and her lips curved up into a wan smile. "I should like to see that."

He returned her smile and once again there was a moment. An understanding.

Before she broke it with a frown, leaning forward in impatience. "But honestly, Damian, how shall I practice here? There is no instrument in sight."

He grinned, reaching out and bopping her nose like she was a child. Her look said she was not amused.

"The fact that there is no instrument here is precisely the point." The carriage rattled as it slowed. "For now we are through with those lessons. Today we focus on your voice."

Her eyes widened and she clapped a hand over her throat. "My voice?"

The voice in question sounded an awful lot like a squeak at the moment.

"Your voice," he repeated slowly, as if she had merely misheard.

"But I can't—" Her protest was cut short as the carriage came to a halt and he swung the door open. Helping her out and then the lady's maid, who'd clearly been trained well to be all but invisible, he led Pru toward the center of excitement.

They headed through a maze of stalls, past a marionette show which was thronged with children, away from the livestock which stunk to high heaven, and bought them each a jam tart before finding a bench for them to sit and watch the action.

The lady's maid hovered nearby, watching them like a hawk. "She could have had a treat too, you know."

Pru shrugged. "I offered. She refused." She eyed the tart in her hands with such longing, he had the sudden urge to snatch it away from her and hold it up in front of his face to see what it would feel like to have her look at him that way.

Stuff and nonsense. He took a bite with a shake of his head, waiting for her to do the same. When she didn't, he nudged her arm. "Is there something wrong with it? I can get you another if you'd prefer—"

"Oh no, there's nothing wrong. I just shouldn't, that's all." She continued to eye the treat as if it were her first love leaving for sea.

He started to scoff, ready to tease her for this rare display of melodrama, but caught himself just in time.

She was not in jest. She was serious. She was debating whether or not to eat the sweets. Her great aunt's horrible words came back to him and he growled low in his throat. "Eat the tart, Pru."

She blinked up at him in surprise. "Pardon me?"

"Eat the tart," he said, gentler this time. "Your aunt has no idea what she's talking about."

"W-what do you mean?" she started.

He rolled his eyes as he shifted to face her. "Tell me, Pru, in all your years living with the Dowager Demon, have you ever seen gentlemen ogling her skin-and-bones body?"

Pru's eyes widened but he was not done.

"Have you ever heard of a man longing for a woman whose stomach is growling and who looks as though she's one missed meal away from starvation?"

Pru blinked, her lips parting in surprise, no doubt at his passion for this particular topic.

"Do you think any man in his right mind would prefer a skin-and-bones miserable old stick like your aunt to someone who is as lush and vivacious and beautiful as you?"

Her eyes were so wide he nearly drowned in them, her lips were so soft and full when they weren't pursed or pressed together in a thin line of disapproval. She was so utterly beguiling when she wasn't—

"That was entirely inappropriate," she breathed.

He choked on a laugh. She was beguiling when she forgot to be priggish Pru. Although, he couldn't quite stop his grin because her words lacked heat and it truly was fantastically diverting to get a rise out of her.

If she were to simper or giggle or heaven forbid flirt after such a phenomenally forward speech like that—

Well, that just wouldn't be Prudence, now would it?

And where would be the fun in that?

He watched her profile as she watched the crowds milling along the path before them. Honestly. When had she become so pretty?

Or had she always been pretty and he'd been too thick to notice?

He nodded to himself. Probably the latter. He'd been a remarkably stupid boy. Well, perhaps not stupid, but definitely selfish. So caught up in his own grief and the wild emotions that came from being uprooted from his comfortable world as the son of society's outcasts. In one moment he'd gone from being a society scandal to the marquess's one and only heir.

Not even his father had believed he would actually inherit

when he'd been the heir presumptive, but as each year passed and his uncle failed to remarry, it was becoming alarmingly clear that he might really be stuck with the title and role he did not want.

If only his uncle's first wife hadn't died. If only he'd had a happy marriage. If only he were anyone but Damian, the thought might not be so abhorrent. But he hadn't been born to this life, and he certainly never wanted it.

He found himself lost in memory until her voice brought him back to the present. "It's been so long since I've been to a fair like this one, I almost forgot they existed."

He let out a short burst of air, halfway between a laugh and a scoff.

"The last time I came to this one—"

"You were miserable," he finished on her behalf. He'd meant it to be teasing. Though she *had* been miserable. Sometimes it had seemed like she was always miserable, and she'd never been content to revel in misery alone.

He glanced over now, expecting to see her rolling her eyes or sighing in exasperation. He was surprised to find her blushing. A mottled red streaked her neck as she dipped her head but her eyes were unfocused, lost in thought.

Lost in memories, just like he'd been.

"That's true," she murmured. "I was miserable."

And all at once, he was ready to kick himself. Of course she'd been miserable. She'd been living with the Dowager Demon back then, too. Her parents had never been around, as far as he knew. She'd been stuck in that awful stuffy house with that horrid, cruel woman.

He winced as the full weight of his childish self-absorption hit him upside the head.

Of course she'd been miserable...and he'd done nothing to help. "I'm sorry, Pru."

THE MISGIVINGS ABOUT MISS PRUDENCE

She whipped her head to the side to face him. "Pardon me?"

He cleared his throat. "I, er...I wanted to apologize."

Her eyes were wide again. Wide and unblinking. "For what? Bringing me here?" She laughed softly. "I'll admit, I'm worried about how I'll explain this to my aunt, but I'm rather pleased to have a break—"

"No," he interrupted. "That wasn't what I meant. I meant that I'm sorry for when we were kids. I'm sorry for teasing you and playing pranks."

Her brows knitted together in confusion. "You're sorry?" Suspicion like he hadn't seen in days lit her eyes. "Why?"

He flinched. "Er..."

Her eyes narrowed.

"It's just that now, as adults, I realize that..." He cleared his throat. Oh curse it. He was toeing the line of pity again, and that would not do. He spit it out quickly. "I realize that your life must not have been easy living with the Dowager Demon and I'm sorry for my part in making your situation more uncomfortable."

She stared at him for such a long time he started to fidget. Then she burst out in a laugh, clapping a hand over her mouth to stifle the sound that brought countless heads turning in their direction, startled birds flying out of the tree overhead, and her chaperone peering over with a glare.

She recovered quickly. "You should not call her that, you know."

He merely tipped his chin in acknowledgement since the chastisement sounded like something she uttered out of habit more than anything.

"Still," he said, a smile teasing his lips as he watched her settle, her whole body seeming to soften with that laugh, her features going from pretty to stunning with that rare display of joy. "You could not have had it easy as a child in that house."

She cast him a quick sidelong look and what he saw there made his heart ache. He felt sorry for Prudence today but the thought of her as an innocent child in that house that held no love, only criticism and scorn…

It made him want to pull her into his arms and tell her all that she was worth, give her everything that she deserved.

The urge came on so fast, so insistent, it left him temporarily stunned and speechless.

"You are hardly to blame for my childhood woes," she said, her smile wry and just a bit cynical. "There is plenty of blame to go around and none of it belongs to you."

He shifted toward her. He had questions that begged to be asked but that were none of his business. He'd heard the rumors about her parents, the dowager duchess's younger sister's wayward daughter. But back then it had all felt so removed. He hadn't bothered to think about what that had been like for her, abandoned by her parents and left with a woman without a maternal bone in her body, the rest of the family taking no interest in her.

"Besides…" Her smile turned gentle. Sweet, almost. It stole his breath right out of his lungs. "You didn't exactly have an easy childhood yourself, now did you?"

The question was rhetorical but he still found himself murmuring, "No. I suppose not."

Just like he'd heard rumors about her parents, he had no doubt she'd heard every detail of the scandal that was his parents. "But," he said, shifting closer. "I was treated kindly by my uncle, and was given every advantage."

She made a noise.

He looked over with a start. "Are you laughing at me?" He honestly wasn't certain whether to be shocked, amused, or offended.

She bit her lip. "My apologies, it's just..." She dropped her voice low in a comical impersonation. *"I was given every advantage."* Her laughter was sweet and melodic. "I'm not certain who you are trying to convince but it was not terribly convincing."

He started to laugh, as well. "You'll think me ungrateful..."

She leaned over, nudging his shoulder with hers in a move that was surprisingly playful. "Go on."

He shrugged. "It's just...I was happier with my parents, that's all."

"Mmm." Her murmur of agreement seemed to say everything and nothing, and it held more than a little bit of wistfulness.

"But Uncle Edward truly was kind. He still is." He flashed her a rueful smile. "He's probably too kind. Some might say he spoils me."

"Really? Who would ever say such a thing?" she asked so mildly that it made him laugh.

"I trust you think it's true."

She shrugged, turning away. "I would have said as such as a child, I'm certain. But I was also terribly jealous of your kind uncle so it's possible I was holding a bit of a grudge."

"A *bit* of a grudge?" he asked, his brows arching in disbelief.

Now it was her turn to laugh at herself, and the fact that she did warmed him all the way through. "Fine. I was extraordinarily jealous of you and your kind household and I treated you badly because of it. Happy now?"

"Very." He wasn't certain if she had changed, or if he had, or if they were only now truly getting to know one another, but hearing her laugh at her own self-righteous image made him shift his view of her again.

At this rate, he wouldn't recognize her come nightfall.

7

This was pleasant. *Too* pleasant.

As far as Prudence was concerned, this entire outing had been too pleasant by far. *Is there such a thing as too pleasant?* She could practically hear Louisa asking that question, but the answer was yes.

Yes, there was.

Because nothing good could come of enjoying Damian's company. Nothing good could come of all this time they'd been spending together unless she suddenly and miraculously became a musical genius.

And unless musical genius was contagious, she couldn't imagine how he would accomplish this by forcing her to eat a jam tart.

She took another bite as they watched the crowds in companionable silence. Not that she particularly minded the tart.

In fact, this treat was the highlight of her week considering she'd eaten the last of the sweets she'd brought back with her from Miss Grayson's ages ago, and her aunt's idea of dessert was an extra serving of vegetables with her dinner.

"Mmm." She let out an embarrassing little moan as she let the last bite melt in her mouth, her eyes closed to savor every last taste sensation. When the last of it was gone, she sighed and opened her eyes to find Damian staring at her.

Not just staring. His eyes were dark and heavy-lidded and so intently focused on her she found herself jerking back with a start, her hand coming up to her lips to ensure there were no embarrassing crumbs or smears of jam causing this sudden interest. "What is it?"

He cleared his throat and shook his head. "I have never seen anyone enjoy anything as much as you have that tart."

She bit her lip, a blush threatening to make her face a mottled mess. "Oh, er..." She looked down at her lap, searching for an excuse for her unbridled joy that did not include explaining Aunt Eleanor's strict diet.

"You should always be eating treats."

"Pardon me?" She looked up in surprise to see him blinking as if coming out of a daze.

"It's nice to see someone enjoy their food," he said, but he wouldn't quite look her way. Then he was dusting crumbs from his hands and standing. "Shall we?"

"Shall we...what?" she asked, still completely perplexed.

His smile was slow and...wicked. There was no other word for it. She no longer believed *him* to be wicked, but when he smiled like that...

A girl could forget.

He reached a hand down to her and after glancing over at her scowling chaperone who would report everything that happened today to Aunt Eleanor, she accepted. He helped her up and linked her arm through his so he was leading them away from the fair, toward the grove of trees on the neighboring farm.

"Where are we going?"

He glanced down at her. "I was not lying when I said we would have a lesson today."

She bit her lip, stealing a glance back at her chaperone who was far enough away not to hear every word, and still… How much had she heard?

Her stomach toppled and turned at the thought.

"Pru?" He peered down at her. "Are you all right?"

She nodded. No. Not really. But right now was not the time to think about the world of trouble she would be in when she got home. Nor was it the time to lose focus of her goal.

To win over her new potential husband. True she did not know him, but that hardly mattered. She couldn't exactly go through the rest of her life without a husband, now could she?

This was what she'd been telling herself for days now, ever since she'd arrived at her aunt's and the reality of her situation had become clear. Mr. Benedict was her one chance to escape. To have a family of her own and a life that wasn't under her aunt's thumb.

She'd managed to forget all that in the safe harmony of Miss Grayson's but being back with her aunt brought with it a stark reality. Being here today and dealing with unwanted childhood memories made that reality that much clearer.

She had been miserable as a child, but she did not wish that for her future. Marriage offered a way out. Her salvation. Her aunt would not pick a cruel man, and by all accounts he was a pleasant fellow.

And yes, she'd asked around. Delilah had met him a few times over the years and she'd said he'd seemed…nice.

On the old side, perhaps, but nice.

Older she could deal with. Nice was what mattered.

And if her nice salvation required that she be able to entertain and perform, why then she would do it. She straightened her shoulders and stiffened her spine. "All right, I am ready," she said when they came to a stop. "Tell me where to begin."

He let her arm go and turned to look at her as her chaperone found a seat nearby on a log and began to crochet. Damian looked too and then tugged her further away. So far they bordered on being out of sight as well as out of earshot.

He placed his hands on her shoulders. "First of all, this needs to go."

She frowned. "What?"

"This…" He shook her shoulders gently and her whole body twisted and turned. "Why are you so stiff? It's unnatural." He pulled back to give her a meaningful look. "Tell me honestly, are you made of wood?"

A small laugh escaped before she could stop it. "I am determined, that's all."

"I see." He eyed her curiously. "Well, you look rather like a soldier heading into battle, and that is not at all the right attitude for this occasion."

"And what occasion is that?"

"My first opportunity to hear you sing."

Her throat closed up entirely. She couldn't have let out a squeak. Her eyes went wide and his did, too.

"What is it?" he asked.

She gave her head a little shake, but she knew her panic must have been written clearly across her face. She wasn't certain how she'd thought he'd begin with her voice but she'd let herself hope they would ease into this. Her teacher at Miss Grayson's had spent nearly a month just working on breathing exercises. Wasn't that where he was supposed to start?

His brows came down as he crossed his arms. "You don't wish to sing."

She shook her head frantically.

"Why not?"

She had to swallow three times before she could get the words out. "Because I can't."

He frowned. "Of course you can. You sang carols along with all the rest of us as a child. I don't recall a particularly lovely voice but I'm certain I would have remembered if you couldn't even carry a tune."

She shook her head again. But that was then, didn't he see? That was back when singing had just been singing. That was before music lessons had become her own personal form of torture.

She shook her head yet again, so hard her teeth were rattling as she kept her lips pinched tightly together.

He stared at her in surprise as she kept her mouth mutinously shut. The stalemate might have gone on forever if he didn't cave first. "Perhaps we should start with something simple. A hymn, perhaps?"

She glowered at him and his look of optimism.

"You cannot tell me you do not sing at church."

She made a *hmph* noise while keeping her mouth shut.

He sighed and crossed his arms. "I thought you were serious about this."

The gentle rebuke had her resolve fading fast. He was right. She'd been determined just a moment ago to make a go of this.

But that was before he'd suggested she sing. The mere thought made her throat feel tight and croaky like a frog. One bad memory after another reared up until she was shaking.

There was nothing more humiliating than her great aunt's displeasure when she failed to hit the right note.

Whatever he saw on her face, Damian relented with another sigh. "All right, let's take this even slower then, hmm?"

She nodded, finally able to take a deep breath. "Perhaps we should try another instrument. I heard the harp was not so difficult to…." Her voice trailed off pathetically at his knowing look.

That was right. She'd nearly forgotten. He'd heard her attempts with the harp. The poor instrument had barely survived the ordeal. "That harp wasn't tuned correctly," she muttered.

Though who she was trying to fool was anyone's guess.

All at once, a wave of bitterness had her scuffing her toes into the dirt at her feet. "Silly music. If I don't marry because of a ridiculous harp, I'll…I'll…" She blew out a long exhale in lieu of a threat.

They both knew it was baseless anyhow. If she did not marry, she would have no power, no leverage, no status…no nothing.

"Silly music," she muttered again, mostly because it felt good to say.

He was watching her closely, an odd mix of sympathy and determination on his face. "You don't have to take your displeasure out on music, you know. Music has no ill-will toward you."

She arched her brows. "You think not? If music were a person, she would be my worst nemesis."

"She, eh?" He moved closer and for a moment she thought he would try that trick again, pulling her into his arms to listen to some inaudible music. Her heart kicked in her chest but she couldn't quite tell if it was excitement or anxiety at the thought.

"Perhaps that is your problem," he continued.

"I do not have a problem." She did. She very clearly did. But a gentleman would not point it out.

"You do have a problem," he said. "And your problem is

with music. I'd say you view music like some extension of your aunt.

She wrinkled her nose.

"Think about it." His voice was insistent and when he reached a hand out to cover her eyes she instinctively pulled back. But he went with her, covering her eyes with his hand. "Picture music."

"This is ridiculous."

"Just do it, Pru."

She sighed loudly, letting all the world know how silly this was, but she did it. She tried to imagine what music would look like as a person.

Her nose crinkled up again as the image came into focus. Oh dear. It did look startlingly similar to her great aunt.

He dropped his hand and when she opened her eyes he looked extraordinarily pleased with himself. "Well?"

She pursed her lips before giving in. "Fine. Music is a woman."

"And?"

She rolled her eyes. "And she resembles my aunt."

He nodded, flashing her that wicked lopsided grin that she knew for certain made young ladies of the *ton* swoon.

Not her, of course. Other ladies.

He leaned forward and lowered his voice. "You should think of music as a man."

She blinked. "A gentleman?"

"A lover."

Her gasp was so loud it startled the birds from the trees and she knew without a doubt that her aunt's spy was watching her like a hawk. With that in mind she took a deep breath and fixed him with a glare. "You shouldn't say such things."

"Why not?" His tone was as smug as his smile. "It is the

truth." He moved, circling her until he was behind her, his hands on her shoulders. "If I recall, once upon a time you were well able to open your mouth and sing a melody. So what changed?"

Her brows went up. Honestly? What had changed? He knew very well what had changed. "It was no longer for fun. Learning to sing became a part of...lessons."

Even she could hear the dread in her voice with that word. Lessons were the bane of her existence. Until Miss Grayson's, that was, but there Miss Grayson had shown such leniency that her aunt wasn't totally wrong.

Her instruction had been lacking when it came to music because Miss Grayson hadn't had the heart to enforce it.

His hands on her shoulders were heavy. Warm. They were...calming. And also not at all calming. How he managed to put her muscles at ease while making her heart race was beyond her.

He shifted her slightly so the chaperone was out of her view, so all she could see was the thicket of trees before her and all she could hear was the sound of laughter and music and children shouting from the fair.

"The only way you can sing is if you relax," he said. His hands moved on her shoulders, massaging the knots there as she tried valiantly not to worry about what the chaperone was thinking, what her aunt would say if she heard.

She jerked away from his touch so quickly she stumbled forward. "I, uh...I cannot relax."

The minute the words were out, she knew how silly they sounded. His smile when she turned to face him was split between understanding and amusement. He glanced over toward the chaperone and turned back with a smile that made her feel like perhaps for once they were on the same side. That maybe they were in on the same joke.

"Perhaps it's time to head back," he said.

Was she imagining it or did he look as though he disliked the idea as much as she?

"We haven't done any sort of lessons," she felt compelled to point out.

He grinned as he helped her over a fallen branch. "Still, we accomplished what I set out to do."

"And what was that?"

His grin was wicked and filled with laughter as he shot a sidelong glance toward the chaperone to ascertain she wasn't close enough to hear. "Steal you away from the evil witch."

Prudence opened her mouth to chide him. He really oughtn't say such things.

But what came out...was a laugh.

8

The sound of Pru's laughter was nice. Melodic and sweet and...lovely.

Now if only he could get her to sing, he had no doubt her voice would be just as sweet. Untrained, of course, and far from perfect. But perfect was overrated, particularly when it came to music.

That was the one lesson he wished to get across to Pru and he wasn't sure how, not after a lifetime of hearing that her very happiness and the course of her life would be determined by whether or not she could achieve perfection.

"Shall we walk back?" he asked on impulse as they reached the carriage.

Pru looked surprised for only a moment before she nodded. "Oh, but Mrs. Hawkins."

He arched his brows. "Who?"

The chaperone a few paces behind him cleared her throat.

Pru lowered her voice. "I am not certain she is fit to walk such a distance."

"Ah," he said. What he meant was, *perfect*. "Then by all means, Mrs. Hawkins shall ride in the carriage—"

He saw the older woman open her mouth to protest but he was already turning to the driver. "You wouldn't mind riding slowly, would you, so as to keep Miss Pottermouth and I in view?"

"Of course not, my lord."

"There you have it," he said, already ushering Mrs. Hawkins toward the carriage as Prudence looked on with a look of alarm.

"Truly?" she asked once they were underway.

"What's wrong?"

"Are you trying to get me killed?" she hissed.

It was official. He absolutely despised the fear he saw in her eyes.

"I told you, Pru." He met her gaze evenly. "I will deal with your aunt."

He'd never been a terribly protective sort. But then again, he'd never had much need to be. He had no younger siblings, no damsels in distress who would turn to him for aid. He eyed Prudence now…

Not that she qualified as a damsel in distress.

But somehow her strength and her forceful demeanor made him want to protect her that much more. He frowned at the ground as he tried to figure out why that was.

"Don't you go getting all grim on me," Prudence murmured beside him.

His head came up with a snap. "Excuse me?"

Her lips twitched upward. "Where will we be if we're both too serious?"

He laughed. "Who said you're too serious?"

She shrugged and he found he couldn't look away from the small smile that hovered on her lips as if she'd forgotten it was there. "My best friend, Delilah. My other friends, Louisa and Addie…"

She looked over and caught his surprise before he could hide it. "Yes, Damian, I do have friends," she said with a roll of her eyes that made him laugh.

"Of course you do," he said.

"Don't be condescending," she said. "If a rakish rogue such as yourself can have some friends then surely a too-serious, sanctimonious goody-two-shoes like me can as well."

He gasped and threw a hand over his heart, feigning shock. "Whoever called you such names?"

She glanced over at him and they both burst out in a laugh that seemed to ease some of the heaviness that had been weighing on him ever since he'd seen that flicker of fear.

"Tell me honestly, Damian," she said after they'd walked in companionable silence for a few moments. "Do you truly think you can make me decent enough of a pianist to be able to perform for my husband-to-be and his family next week without humiliating myself?"

"No," he said promptly. Her face fell and he nudged her lightly. "You will be able to sing, however."

She widened her eyes. "You haven't even heard me sing."

"I know you can carry a tune. I can work with that."

She eyed him oddly. "You have a lot of confidence in your abilities."

He shrugged. "Haven't you ever found something you're particularly good at?"

She tilted her head to the side in thought before nodding. He itched to ask what it was, to hear her talk about her accomplishments and her skills. But right now she needed his reassurance, and that he could give. "Well then, rest assured that my talents lie in music."

She opened her mouth to protest but he cut her off.

"I realized that while I enjoy making music, I enjoy bringing it out in others even more."

"Bringing it out," she repeated quietly. "That's an odd way of putting it."

"It's how I see it," he said. "Everyone has music in them. Like I said the other day. It's everywhere, all the time. It's in us." He clamped his mouth shut before he could say much more. Already he felt ridiculous for being so passionate about the topic, but these past two years he'd stopped trying to fight the pull toward this particular obsession.

Unlike drinking and gambling, his passion for music caused himself and others no harm. It was now his one vice, his only freedom in a life where words like obligation and duty were slowly starting to wear away at his soul.

"How did you become so interested in music?" she asked.

He hesitated, scuffing at the dirt beneath their feet. The farther they got from the center of town, the less crowded the road. It was almost possible to forget their escort which rode slowly behind them. For a moment he could actually pretend they were alone. Maybe that was why he let the truth slip out. "It is all I have left of my parents."

At her silence he continued, his gaze fixed on his feet. "My earliest memories were of singing, of dancing, of playing music that made the entire household rattle." A smile tugged at his lips at the memory.

"That must have been a wonderful house to be a child," she said, her voice little more than a whisper.

He nodded. "It was. Although it wasn't all perfect. I'm sure you've heard about how my father ran off with a gypsy woman."

She blinked in surprise at his candor, and he grinned. "It's all right. What's a few secrets between friends, hmm?"

"Is that what we are?" she asked.

His smile faltered when he looked at her. "Aren't we?"

She didn't answer, and he was glad. Because now that the question was out there, he wasn't certain how he wished her to answer. Were they friends?

He wasn't certain what he felt toward her counted as friendship. But it wasn't the same antagonistic rivalry from their youth either. Whatever this was he was starting to feel for her, it was strong and it was sweet and it was....terrifying.

He looked away quickly, afraid of what she might be seeing in his expression.

"Tell me more," she said. "What was not so perfect about your childhood home?"

"The whispers. The gossip." He shrugged. "I knew from the time I could walk that we did not fit in, not the way we ought. My parents never tried to shield me from it. They did not revel in being a scandal, and I know that it caused quite a bit of pain, particularly for my mother. But they cared more about each other, more about our family, than they cared about what society thought." He swallowed down a wave of emotions as old memories came to light. "I think they would have been content to live as outcasts for the rest of their lives, which..." He scratched the back of his head self-consciously as he finished. "I suppose they did."

Silence fell and it felt too heavy for such a fine day.

"Anyhow," he continued in a lighter tone. "Music was the one thing I brought with me from home and I suppose I never wanted to let it go. I suppose that sounds ridiculous, doesn't it?"

Her voice was soft, sad. "It sounds lovely."

He glanced up at her and caught it. A rare glimpse of vulnerability. His heart jerked in his chest and his lungs seized, and the truth was out before he could stop it. "*You* are lovely."

She blinked, her eyes widening as his words registered. Blushing, she looked down. "Thank you, but you needn't say things like that."

He opened his mouth to argue, to tell her that it was the truth, but she was already walking ahead. They'd reached the drive leading to her aunt's formidable manor and they slowed as the carriage rolled past them to the front door.

"Let us go around this way," he said.

She arched a knowing brow. "Trying to avoid my aunt?"

He laughed. "Something like that."

The truth was, he wanted just a few more moments alone with her like this. Moments when she was relaxed and defenseless, when her guard was down and her spirits were up.

Moments when she was herself. Not trying to be some perfect version of herself and live up to anyone else's expectations. All at once he had a surge of gratitude toward his parents and his uncle. He might have known grief, and he understood better than most how it felt to be on the outside looking in, but in his home he had always been treated with love, despite his imperfections.

He'd been seen for who he was, not who he was expected to be.

"It is a shame you won't be able to continue with your music tutoring." Prudence's words brought him back to the moment.

"What do you mean?"

She arched a brow. "It is exceptional as it is that your uncle allows you to pursue this hobby of yours," she said. "But when you become the Marquess of—"

"Who says that I will?" He'd meant it to sound light and teasing, but it fell flat. Instead, he merely sounded defensive. "Who says that I wish to be?"

She stared at him in surprise as they rounded the far

side of the house toward the glass doors of the music room. "I know you've hinted at it before, but I thought you were teasing. You can't mean that..." She stopped and stared. "You truly do not wish to become the next Marquess of Ainsley?"

He opened his mouth, ready to give one of the pat answers he was used to throwing out there when the topic of his status came up. But one look at her genuine curiosity and the quip died in his throat. "No," he said simply.

"No?" Her eyes grew so wide it looked painful. "But...everyone wants power, wealth, and status."

"Yes, but you see, what everyone else wants has no bearing on my own wishes for my future. And I have no wish to be Marquess."

"But why not?" she asked, still gaping adorably.

He grinned at the rare sight of her not knowing everything about everything. "Why would I want that? I already told you that I was born an outsider, raised an outsider. The peerage and the gentry never had a use for me before my father died, why should I wish to join their ranks now?"

She opened her mouth and then shut it as they continued walking. Finally, she huffed as they neared the doors, pausing to face him. "That seems like an odd sort of logic. Don't you wish to throw their disdain in their faces by becoming a powerful member of society?"

He frowned as he thought it over. "Not particularly."

This seemed to vex her, which amused him. "But why not?"

"Because what would that change? What they think of me will likely never alter. And I don't particularly care what they think of me anyway." He tossed his hands in the air. "My parents taught me well that what other people say and do doesn't matter as much as our own compass."

"A compass?" she echoed.

"Yes. Doing what we feel is right. Following our intuition, our instincts..." He hesitated for a moment. "Our hearts."

"Well, that..." She bit her lip, her gaze darting left and right as she seemed to chase her thoughts. "That's very romantic."

He laughed. Was it? He didn't think so. But even so... "How do you manage to make romantic sound like a curse word?"

Her lips twitched up as she shrugged. "Just as I know about your family scandal, I'm certain you know of mine."

He nodded slowly.

"So you see, romance for me is not something I particularly admire." She sniffed and the priggish girl he knew was back in full force, and the sight of her made him want to laugh and tease until she was either giggling or smacking him.

Instead, he imitated her with a haughty sniff. "*It's not something I particularly admire.* Really, Pru, you sound like your aunt."

She choked on a laugh. "I don't! I merely think romance and love and all that is just an excuse for being selfish."

He nodded, his gaze searching hers for more. For something he couldn't name. "I see. But I, on the other hand, see talk of duty and obligation as just an excuse to avoid being brave."

She gasped and jerked back as if he struck her. "That's a horrible thing to say."

He thought that over. "Is it?"

"It is." She sounded so vehement he thought it best not to argue the point further. While he'd discovered that he truly loved bickering with Pru—possibly more than was sane—he had no wish to mar this day which had started so terribly and ended... Well, perfectly.

He wondered if she was thinking something similar when

she glanced wistfully toward the house. "Are we done with today's lesson then or...or is there more?"

He was done. It should be done. But he found he didn't want this to end.

Reaching for her hand, he tugged her away from the door and toward the gardens. "My dear, we have only just begun."

9

Her heart was thumping wildly as she let him lead her away from her home, from her aunt...from her chaperone.

Prudence never broke the rules. She lived by rules, led her life by the compass of propriety, and prided herself on being everything that her parents were not.

Dutiful. Obedient. Proper.

So why on earth was she letting him lead her astray? Why could she not bring herself to dig in her heels or say something biting?

And why on earth was her heart on a mission to leap out of her chest? With her free hand she clutched her chest just as he finally came to a stop at the edge of the gardens. Not entirely hidden by the hedges that surrounded them, but not in clear view of the main house either.

Her chaperone, the servants, even her aunt, were within shouting distance, and possibly even watching her right now.

As far as decency went, she was walking a fine line. She was courting trouble.

She ought to stop this. Now, with her future at stake and

spinsterhood looming if she failed to win over Mr. Benedict—this was absolutely *not* the time to become a rebel.

Damian's lips curved up into that wicked grin that used to drive her mad as a child.

It still drove her mad, but this madness wasn't the same.

Her heart went wild again, racing in her chest like she was running for her life and not standing here with her music tutor.

No, this madness wasn't the same at all.

"Are you ready to sing for me yet?" he asked.

She blinked. He was serious. "No. I shall never be ready to sing."

He looked around pointedly. "That nasty old crone isn't here to watch you like a hawk, we are far from the stifling atmosphere in your aunt's unwelcoming home." He arched his brows. "Is it me you are uncomfortable with?"

She opened her mouth and closed it abruptly. *No.* The answer was no, but that was alarming. While he made her heart race and a tension seemed to fall around them whenever they were alone, this sensation wasn't unpleasant. It wasn't nerves or intimidation or fear that he would judge her.

It was something else entirely. And that…

That was more frightening to admit than anything else she could say.

"Ah," he said with a knowing tone. "You are worried about what I might think, hmm?"

She pursed her lips. No. That wasn't it at all. But before she could say as much, he was singing.

He was singing loudly and enthusiastically and…inappropriately. The song he was singing was some sort of crude tavern tune that had her cheeks burning even as she burst out in a laugh. "What are you doing?"

He took a deep breath and started on the next verse

before she leaned forward and clapped a hand over his mouth. "Stop it," she said through her laughter.

His eyes still danced with amusement and her cheeks hurt from grinning but as their laughter faded, the tension returned and she dropped her hand from his mouth as if he'd burned her.

Turning away quickly, she took a deep breath to calm the butterflies in her stomach that she knew without a doubt had nothing to do with singing and everything to do with this bizarre connection she felt whenever he was near.

Physically it was impossible to ignore or deny. Even now, when he was out of her direct sight, she could feel his body coming closer as though she had some sort of sixth sense. Emotionally, too, she felt it. Never before had she felt so seen. So exposed.

So vulnerable.

Maybe it was because he knew of her past and had been acquainted with her for so long, but not even her closest friends seemed to understand her the way that he did.

It was unnerving.

"Now it is your turn." His low voice behind her made her stiffen.

"I-I'm too embarrassed," she said. "Even singing that horrible song, you have a lovely voice and you know it."

He chuckled. "Then keep your back to me if that makes you feel better, but know that I am not here to judge. And nothing you could do, say, or sing would ever make me think less of you, Pru."

She blinked as a surge of unexpected emotions had her throat aching and her eyes stinging. That was absolutely the nicest thing anyone had ever said to her.

Ever.

The sincerity in his voice left her speechless but his hands on her shoulders made her stiffen again.

"Easy, Pru," he soothed, his hands rubbing her shoulders, massaging the tight muscles there until she felt like hot butter, ready to melt at his feet. "There," he said. "Just relax, and you will be fine. Like I said, as a child you knew how to hold a tune. You have a natural ear for music, you've just had it beaten out of you."

She cast a quizzical glance over her shoulder. "Beaten out of me?"

He nodded, utterly serious despite her wry tone. "Your aunt turned something that should be lighthearted and joyous into something unpleasant." His gaze roamed over her. "A punishment, I'd imagine."

Her stomach turned at the mere memory of music lessons that ended in scoldings or bedtime without supper.

"Your aunt made music so unpleasant that you tense up at the mere mention of singing or performing. But it is impossible to play any instrument well if you are overthinking every movement at every turn." He gently turned her head so she was staring at the garden rather than at him. "And you cannot sing at all if you are frozen with fear."

Frozen with fear. The words resonated inside of her as if they'd just struck a bell. She had been living in fear. In some ways, she supposed she was so accustomed to this state that she forgot. She'd grown so used to it that she'd become numb to it.

But now he'd called her out on it and she found herself shaken to her core.

He moved to stand in front of her and tipped her chin up to meet his gaze. "If you let go of that fear and relax, I have no doubt that you will be amazing."

She arched her brows dubiously.

His lips curved up. "Fine. I have no doubt you will be passable."

A laugh slipped out before she could stop it and he smiled in return. "You should do that more often."

"What?"

He shrugged, his hand dropping. "Smile. Laugh."

She looked away in discomfort. Was she really so very stiff that a laugh was something to remark upon?

Yes. She could practically hear Louisa laughing as she shouted it in her ear. *Yes!*

She pursed her lips with a scowl and made a mental note to tell Delilah how Louisa had become her own personal spectre, haunting her in broad daylight.

"Right. Before you can overthink it, let us do this." He spun her around abruptly so her back was to his chest. His arm wrapped around her waist until his hand was covering her belly.

She froze.

No, she melted at the touch. Heat seemed to sear her insides as he held her close, his voice a low murmur in her ear. "Take a deep breath in so you can see my hand rise and fall."

She did as she was told, too stunned by the intimacy to protest.

"Good," he murmured. "Now sing."

She blinked at the shrubbery before her. "Sing what?"

She could feel his shrug. "Anything. Whatever is familiar."

Shifting a bit she wracked her brain for something that she knew well and settled on an old-fashioned song that her first nurse used to sing to her as a lullaby. She opened her mouth, her throat threatened to choke her.

"Relax. Be yourself," he whispered in her ear, his arm closing tighter around her in an odd sort of comforting embrace. "I've got you."

With a sigh she began, and the sound of her own voice

filling the silence startled her. How long had it been since she'd heard herself sing?

Too long.

Not long enough.

The act of singing awoke a myriad of emotions she couldn't quite name. While trying to remember the words and stay on key, it was difficult to dwell on these sensations, the old feelings she'd thought she'd buried.

She'd thought she'd killed.

They weren't dead and they weren't even gone. They were right here, just under the surface, it seemed. They came to life as she sang and...they were overwhelming. She found herself grateful for Damian's tight grip, and when he turned her around as her voice trailed off, she was stunned to discover she'd been crying.

It wasn't until he lifted a hand and wiped away her tears that she realized it.

"Pru..." The tenderness in his eyes was nearly her undoing.

She shook her head quickly with a sniff. "I'm all right."

"You're better than all right," he said with a grin that helped to wipe away the heaviness of the moment. "You were perfect."

She snorted in disbelief and that made his grin widen. "I mean it. You sounded lovely when you forgot to be a stuck-up goody two shoes."

Choking on a laugh, she swatted his arm away when he went to brush more tears from her cheeks. "Perhaps I am a bit of a goody two shoes, but I hardly see how that's a bad thing."

He laughed. "Don't you?"

"No."

He tilted his head to the side to study her. "Tell me, Pru, haven't you ever once wanted to rebel?"

She opened her mouth to say 'no' but it wouldn't come out. The question threw her more than she wanted to admit. Instead, she sniffed. "You do enough rebelling for the both of us."

He laughed and she caught a whiff of understanding. He knew what she was doing, he knew that she was deflecting, and he wasn't going to push her. "You're probably right. I do like to push the boundaries."

She looked around at their current secluded surroundings and shook her head with a mix of awe and horror. "What is it about being with you that has me wanting to break the rules, too?"

She felt the change in him. A stiffening or a tension as he gazed down at her. "Do I do that to you?"

She nodded, unable to meet his searching gaze. "You do."

She wasn't entirely certain what she was admitting to, but she felt certain that he knew. There was some undercurrent here that made her feel as if she was on shaky ground while he seemed to be more confident than ever.

"You make me want to do the right thing," he said, so quietly she almost missed it. She glanced up quickly and saw the dark swirl of emotions in his eyes and it took her breath away.

"You make me want to…" He shook his head, tearing his gaze away as he took a deep breath, a familiar teasing smile curving his lips. "You make me want to play the role of savior."

She blinked in surprise, torn between this impossibly sweet sensation that made her chest ache and a sinking sensation in the pit of her belly as his words registered. "You feel so sorry for me that you wish to play knight in shining armor, is that it?"

Surprise flared in his eyes but he caught himself quickly. "That wasn't what I meant."

Now she was the one to look away. Of course he felt sorry for her. She'd seen the way he'd looked at her hands where her aunt had struck her as though she were still a child. She'd seen the way he'd been looking at her ever since she'd fainted at his feet.

As though she were pitiable.

And perhaps she was.

The thought made her more irritated than sad. She hated being pitied. It wasn't as though she'd been given such a terrible lot in life. Just one without many options.

And that was something a gentleman like him would never understand.

So perhaps it stood to reason that he would feel sorry for her. Maybe to such an extent that he'd feel compelled to help her, to do right by her…

The thought had her fighting tears all over again and this time she definitely could not explain why. "We should head back before my chaperone tells my aunt we have gone missing."

She headed toward the music room doors without waiting for a response.

10

*D*amian hurried after her, his head spinning from the moment that had just occurred.

He had the unnerving sensation that in one afternoon his life had been flipped upside down and he no longer knew which way was up and which was down.

Or no, perhaps it hadn't happened in an instant. Maybe this sensation had been taking root for days now, ever since he'd spotted the now-grown Prudence in her aunt's drawing room. Maybe it had taken root and been growing slowly but surely this entire time.

But that did not change the fact that this afternoon the new sensations had hit him upside the head. His skull still felt like it was ringing after the intimate moment when he'd held her in his arms, when she'd relaxed enough to sing, when her voice had carried more emotions than she could ever realize. She'd laid herself bare in that moment, and the way he'd felt about her...

It had been painful.

Crushing.

The wave of emotion had been so intense it had shifted something inside of him forever.

And now she was running away.

"Pru, please wait," he said, finally catching up to her as she reached the veranda outside the music room doors. "Don't walk away from me just yet."

She paused with her back to him and for a moment he scrambled with what to say.

"Please," he said.

She turned slowly, her gaze wary. "What is it that you want, Damian?"

His breath caught at the searching look in her eyes as much as at the unexpectedness of her question. He suspected she didn't just mean right now at this very moment. But what did he want, in the long run?

"I want to forge my own path, I suppose." He stepped closer, grateful when she didn't rush away from him again. "If I had my way, my uncle would remarry, he'd sire an heir and I could be free to live how I wished."

He expected the sort of pursed-lip scowl he was used to from her whenever he spoke about stepping outside of her precious society and its rules. Instead he caught a flicker of yearning. Perhaps even desire.

But it was tampered by something sad. Regret, maybe, or longing for something she could not have.

"What would you do if you were no longer the heir presumptive?" she asked.

He licked his lips, oddly nervous. He'd never spoken about this to anyone before but after the way she'd opened up to him—knowingly or not—he couldn't keep it from her.

"This," he said with a rueful smile, gesturing vaguely to the two of them. "I'd love to pursue music as a career. Perhaps make it something more meaningful, maybe…" He cleared his throat and glanced away. "Maybe open a conservatory one day."

His gaze darted back and he snuck a peek at her expression, waiting to see amusement or criticism...but what he found was a thoughtful look as she thought it over. "Yes, I could see that," she said.

He laughed in surprise. "You could?"

She shrugged. "Of course. You're passionate about music and you have the connections to make it a success, not to mention the wealth to fund such a venture."

His eyes widened in shock. "You actually think it could work. That I..." He cleared his throat, resisting the urge to tug on his suddenly too-tight cravat as a bewildering surge of nerves made him fidget like a schoolboy. "You truly think that I could do such a thing?"

Her brows came down, her expression so serious it made him want to hug her. She was oddly adorable when she was so serious like this.

"Of course you could," she said.

"I don't know. I don't have much experience managing something like that or running a business of any sort."

Her lips quirked up in an endearing smile. "I always thought I'd be rather good at running a business."

He grinned. "Oh really?"

Now it was her turn to squirm and he delighted in her discomfort. She looked to the ground, her arms crossing defensively. "I've always been good with numbers and my friends at the finishing school are forever teasing me about my managing ways." She peeked up at him. "Silly, isn't it?"

"Not at all," he said quickly. "I could easily imagine it."

"You could?" She sounded so surprised but before he could continue, she added, "Yes, well, I suppose my skills will be an asset as a wealthy merchant's wife."

The sudden reminder of her arrangement made his

throat feel parched and his chest hollow. And then she looked at him and he knew his chest wasn't hollow at all.

It was full.

It was aching.

And his heart felt like it might burst with feeling.

She looked away first and he had to wonder. Did she feel it, too?

She must. But she was shifting toward the doors, her expression already hardening, her chin setting with determination, or perhaps resignation.

He moved toward her before he could stop himself. He didn't want to let her go, he didn't want this moment to end, and that... That was alarming. "Pru," he said before he stopped to think. He had no idea what he was going to say.

He felt like he had everything to say and nothing all at once. He wanted to tell her she did not need to live up to her aunt's impossible standards, but she would not believe him. He wanted to tell her that this gentleman ought to appreciate her for the woman she was, because who she was was perfect. He had this desire to make her see that she deserved so much more than her great aunt could ever know.

He also had the strangest desire to tell her more of his own wishes, to hear her thoughts, to know her opinions, but this wasn't the time or the place.

He reached for her, grasping her arms and tugging her close. The flicker of shock and heat in her eyes the only giveaway that she felt it too, whatever it was that flowed between them.

He wanted to close the distance, to touch his lips to hers, to feel her breath against his skin.

"What are you doing?" she asked, her eyes wide.

He fought the urge to pull her closer still, because yes, he wanted to hold her but more than anything he ached to know what it was that *she* wanted. What she desired when she forgot about her duties and obligations. What she dreamt of when no one else was around and her imagination was free to roam.

He wanted to know her deepest desires, but he was too afraid to ask. Because right now, with that little tip of her chin, he knew that she was readying herself for the life she thought she was destined for.

You deserve so much more.

But the moment from before was gone. The vulnerable young lady he'd caught a glimpse of was once more tucked away beneath the prim and proper prig persona that he knew now was mostly an act.

So instead, he stood there. Frozen. His hands on her arms as his mind raced to figure out what was going on here and what to make of this pull his felt, and the answering tug of fear that said to walk away.

His entire being torn between pulling her close and pushing her away.

He never did get to decide.

Her aunt made the decision for him.

"Here she is," she announced loudly as she threw open the doors. She stopped short at the sight of them alone, standing so close it was nearly an embrace, his hands on her arms...

He dropped them just as her gaze fell to take in the odd proximity.

"What is going on here?" she hissed, but her fierce glare faded, replaced by something more frightening. Something he'd never once seen before.

A smile.

It looked foreign and painful, and it frightened him more than her scowls and glares ever could. "Ah, Lord Damian," she said, her voice scratchy as if it was resisting this sweet tone.

He glanced at Pru who looked equally confused...and terrified.

"I was just telling our guests about you." She stepped aside, revealing an audience who'd no doubt seen their closeness, not to mention the fact that they were alone.

He swallowed down a protective urge to shove Prudence behind him, away from the scrutiny of her aunt and these two gentlemen he did not recognize.

"Allow me to introduce you to Sir William and his nephew, Mr. Benedict."

The names took a moment to register and as he went through the proper motions, he saw the change in Prudence. He couldn't *not* notice her, it seemed. Even while taking in the not-unattractive but not exactly handsome Mr. Benedict before him, he was acutely aware of Prudence. Her posture, her stiffness, the way she'd retreated back to her old self.

The one that wasn't really her at all.

He knew that now.

But did anyone else?

11

*P*rudence glanced down the dining hall toward Mr. Benedict. He wasn't *awful*, so that was something. She toyed with her spoon as a new course was laid before her, trying and failing to keep her gaze from darting over to the man who might possibly be her husband someday.

After an excruciatingly proper and awkward introduction, they had all retreated inside. It seemed there had been a miscommunication along the way. They'd long since intended to arrive today, and she was the only one who'd been unaware of the change in plans.

I was supposed to have another week! That was what kept rushing through her head all afternoon as she watched her husband-to-be and his uncle be escorted to their rooms, and then as she watched far more warily as Damian asked for a moment alone with her great aunt.

Let me deal with her. That was what he'd been saying all day, and now he had and she had no idea what he'd said or how her aunt had taken it.

She turned her gaze down toward the soup before her

and wondered how on earth she was going to get through this meal without screaming.

First Damian and her aunt locked in a room together and then hushed conversations with her aunt and their guests.

And now this.

A tense meal at which everyone but her was allowed to speak.

She had the feeling that her life was happening without her. Her aunt, these gentlemen—even Damian—they were all planning and plotting her life as though she were a doll.

Aren't you, though? Once again it was Louisa in her head.

She scowled at her soup. Why was it always Louisa taunting her. Not mean-spiritedly, just in that way that Louisa had of teasing. Always calling everyone out for their foibles and their facades.

Rather like Damian, come to think of it.

Prudence dipped her spoon into the soup and tried to take a sip, though the rich creamy texture turned her already queasy stomach.

Oddly enough, she missed Louisa right now. Though she might tease, she'd also break this unbearable tension if she were here. And Addie, if she were here, would be casting Prudence supportive, furtive smiles filled with sympathy and understanding. Miss Grayson—oh, her heart ached to think of how the ever-maternal and kind Miss Grayson would make her feel as though all would be well if she were here.

But it was Delilah she missed most of all. Dee would know what to do. She never took a back seat to her own life. Even now she was probably working with her dashing fiancé to orchestrate some sort of plan to take control of her father's estate and get vengeance on her stepmother who'd wronged her.

She certainly wouldn't be sipping soup in silence as the people around her planned the rest of her life.

Prudence dropped her soup spoon with a clatter. Not entirely on purpose, but it still served to break the unceasing silence that was fraught with tension. For her, at least.

All eyes were on her and her mouth went dry. Her aunt's withering stare, in particular, seemed to be boring a hole into her skull. "Mr Benedict, I trust your sister is well," she said.

She had no reason to believe his sister was well or otherwise. She'd only met the woman once and had barely exchanged three words. But it was the best she could come up with at the moment.

"Oh yes, quite well."

Sir William launched into speech then and Prudence was finally able to relax a bit as he filled the air with boring talk of their other relations. His nephew, meanwhile, watched her with an intensity that was alarming.

"Isn't it odd that Lord Damian has taken to tutoring young ladies in music?" he mused as another silence descended.

Prudence tensed even though his tone was as mild as his expression. He hardly seemed put out by the fact that his potential bride had been caught alone with a known rake.

That was...good, she supposed. It wouldn't do to have a jealous hothead for a husband. Not that he had anything to be jealous about.

Damian might have been exceedingly handsome and extraordinarily dashing, particularly when compared to the plain, one might say bland-looking Mr. Benedict, but no one in his right mind would believe that he was interested in *her*. Not as anything more than a student, at least.

Aunt Eleanor's laughter was jarring. "You know how eccentric these young lads can be. Always wanting to make a name for themselves."

Mr. Benedict's sniff seemed to indicate that he did indeed understand. Or perhaps he was merely coming down with a cold. Either way, the sniff rubbed Prudence the wrong way.

"But you know," Aunt Eleanor continued. "Lord Damian is quite in demand as a tutor. He only takes on special cases." She flicked a damning gaze in Prudence's direction. "Those who deserve extra attention."

"Ah." His face lit with pleasure as he turned to Prudence. "You take your studies seriously then, that is good to hear."

"Mmm," she murmured. "Quite."

"You have a special interest in music, I take it?" Mr. Benedict looked so eager at this news she was stumped as to how to answer.

"I, er…" Her mind flashed back to her lesson this morning, the way Damian's face seemed to glow with happiness as he talked about music. "I believe music can be quite powerful."

She expected this man who apparently so revered music to agree, but to her surprise he tipped his head from side to side. "Personally, I find music to be a silly and frivolous waste of one's time. But for a young lady it's a necessity, I assume."

Her brows arched and she had to resist the urge to shoot Aunt Eleanor with a questioning look. She'd made it seem as though Mr. Benedict held a woman's ability to play the pianoforte above all else.

She ought to have known that her aunt was exaggerating. By the sounds of it, this man was more sensible than she'd given him credit. "My best subject has always been mathematics," she offered.

He stared at her for a long moment. Then he laughed, exchanging an amused look with his uncle. "Mathematics? Whatever will you use that for?"

She straightened, ready to reply, but her aunt spoke first. "Young ladies are often encouraged to learn their numbers and figures. It's highly useful when managing a household, I assure you."

Prudence stared at her aunt with an open mouth. Had Aunt Eleanor just...stood up for her?

But Aunt Eleanor chose that moment to shoot her a glare that made her insides wither. Prudence had spoken out of turn, that glare seemed to say. And now her aunt was doing her best to fix the situation.

"Is that what they're teaching young girls at these finishing schools nowadays?" Mr. Benedict asked with a sneer that made Prudence squirm in her seat.

Aunt Eleanor merely took a sip of her soup.

"All a young lady needs to know to run a household is how to add two plus two, isn't that right, Sir William?"

His uncle laughed heartily. Aunt Eleanor did not.

"What else are they teaching Miss Pottermouth at that school of hers?" Sir William asked.

"Never fear, gentlemen. The ladies who run the school have their priorities in order," she said with a sniff. "Why, several of the girls there have recently become engaged. Isn't that right, Prudence?"

"Yes, Aunt Eleanor," she murmured dutifully.

Her aunt rattled off the engagements, which sounded impressive indeed. An earl. A marquess. The second son of a duke.

Prudence had to fight to keep her posture straight as she listened to her friends' epic romances reduced to a list of titles and connections.

It wasn't as though she were jealous. She wasn't. Aside from her great aunt, her connections were not so very great. And being the daughter of a scandal hardly helped her situation. She'd never had hopes for a great marriage or even dreamt of a title.

She glanced over at Mr. Benedict who was clearly impressed with her friends and their newfound status.

No, she was absolutely content to marry a wealthy merchant. It was the best she could hope for and she knew it.

Mr. Benedict turned to her. "My, you are quite well connected, aren't you?"

Her smile felt wan. "I suppose I am."

"Now you are being modest, dear." Her great aunt's voice was grating in its falseness. "Why, just this afternoon Lord Damian assured me that he and his uncle would be joining us for a music recital so we can all hear how well his lessons have been working."

"The Marquess of Ainsley will be joining us?" Sir William's eyes were wide with shock. He and Mr. Benedict both looked suitably impressed.

Her aunt's gaze was fixed on her and Prudence was certain she'd seen her start.

Recital? Tomorrow?

And Damian would be there? She couldn't even bring herself to think about the marquess or her potential husband, not now when pieces were falling into place.

So that was how he'd handled her aunt. With a bribe. He'd no doubt used his position and his uncle's to ensure that her aunt was appeased.

Prudence toyed with her spoon. She wasn't certain whether to be amused, impressed, or annoyed. Was that how he handled all situations? How many times had he been caught alone with a student and talked his way out of it by using his uncle's status?

"Miss Pottermouth, is everything all right?" Mr. Benedict asked.

"Oh, yes. Of course." She smiled brightly, as if that would make it true. Meanwhile her insides were twisting and churning and she could not be sure whether it was at the idea of performing or the thought of Damian with other young ladies.

"Well, I for one am looking forward to hearing this performance tomorrow evening," Mr. Benedict said with a smile in her direction that felt so patronizing it bordered on insulting. "I may find music and the arts a frivolous pastime but having a wife who can entertain clients and colleagues in the drawing room is a fact of life for a man like me." As he said this, he puffed his chest out to a magnificent degree.

Prudence felt the words like a blow. No, it was his tone. So sanctimonious. So smug. So...so...so similar to her own.

Was that how she sounded?

The air rushed out of her lungs as she thought back to all the times Louisa had used those very same words to describe her.

She'd always been so sure of herself. So confident in her skills—well, all except one. She'd always known that she worked hard to be the perfect wife, that she did her very best to be the perfect niece her aunt expected.

And right here, right now, it all seemed to be for naught. Because she hadn't mastered the one skill that mattered most to this man.

After dinner, her aunt cornered her alone. "Do not think for one second that you are excused for the way you behaved earlier," she snarled when Mr. Benedict and Sir William were out of earshot.

"P-pardon?"

Her aunt's expression was hard, her tone unyielding. "Your behavior was a disgrace," she hissed. "Taking Lord Damian off alone like that. Throwing yourself at him like some sort of—"

"I did not—"

"Do not interrupt me, girl." She took a step closer and lowered her voice. "Do you think you can do better than Mr.

Benedict, is that it? You, the daughter of a scandal? Do you think that just because you are distantly related to a peer you have a right to that status yourself?"

"N-no, Aunt—"

"Lord Damian can do better than a girl like you, and if you have your sights on the marquess, then let me tell you—"

"I don't have my sights on anyone." She said it too loudly and she and her aunt both paused to glance over at the gentlemen.

"Keep your voice down and don't cause me any more problems." Her aunt was already fixing a frightening smile on her face as she turned back toward the others. "And you'd better prove Lord Damian correct tomorrow evening."

"Prove him correct? W-what did he say?"

Aunt Eleanor's smile faded with a sniff of disdain. "He said you were perfect. Ha!" She let out a bark of laughter that held no humor, only insult. "Can you imagine?"

"He said that…?" Her voice trailed off because it was quickly becoming clear that she was talking to herself. Her aunt had already set off to give orders to the staff and Prudence was left to stand there and wonder.

Just what exactly had Damian said to her aunt earlier today?

12

Uncle Edward rubbed at his temples as early afternoon light filtered in through the study's open window. The autumn air was crisp and refreshing, but it did not seem to be helping his uncle's headache. "And you two were alone?"

Damian winced. He had a suspicion that he was responsible for this particular headache. No matter how he phrased it, his uncle kept coming back to that one point. "As I said before, we'd had a chaperone but she'd taken the carriage back and—"

"And you were alone," his uncle finished.

Damian sighed. He wasn't sure why he was still trying. Possibly because he didn't want anyone getting the wrong impression. Not about Pru, at least.

Guilt nagged at him, and something else, too. Something far more elusive and way more terrifying. He'd been so close to Prudence, and when her aunt and those others came outside, nothing had been going on between them, but...

He'd wanted to kiss her.

He'd thought about it.

Oh, who was he trying to fool? If he'd been out there alone with her for one second longer, he would have kissed her. There was no doubt about it, and there was certainly no thinking involved.

How could he not kiss her when she was looking at him like that? Like it was just the two of them. Like they were a team, on the same side, like she might actually need him and his help. Like he had something to offer.

Uncle Edward rubbed his eyes. "You need to be more careful, Damian."

"I know, I know. But it was my fault, not hers. And the only way I could make it right—"

"Was to offer me up as a sacrifice at some poor girl's music recital?" His uncle looked pained.

Damian winced again. "Well, when you phrase it like that…"

His uncle gave a short laugh but it trailed off as his eyes narrowed with suspicion. Damian was starting to be very familiar with that look. "This isn't another one of your attempts to find me a new wife, now is it?"

Damian did his best impersonation of a man offended. "I would never."

His uncle raised a brow.

"I would never…so soon after my last attempt," he amended, making them both grin.

Edward shook his head. "You're the only person I know who wants to run from the peerage."

"I'm the only person you know. Period." He heaved a weary sigh that sounded remarkably similar to his uncle's. "You're so mired down in work and obligations, you never meet anyone new. Perhaps there is a wonderful young lady out there who is perfect for you—"

"Damian," his uncle growled in warning.

Damian sighed again, this time in exasperation. His uncle

had always been tight lipped about his first marriage, which ended when his wife died shortly before Damian was brought to live with his uncle. All he knew for certain was that his uncle wasn't keen on trying again, even if that meant the title passed on to him—the notorious half-gypsy nephew who had no desire to take on the role.

But, that was a battle for another day. For right now, all that mattered was making good on his promise to the Dowager Demon to ensure his uncle was in attendance this evening. Otherwise, he hated to think what sort of trouble Prudence would be in with the old bat.

Only talk of his powerful uncle and his slightly exaggerated interest in Prudence had smoothed over her obvious anger at their impropriety.

"You will come, Uncle, won't you?" He leaned forward eagerly and watched as his uncle relented right in front of his eyes.

"Fine. What better way to spend an evening than listening to a novice musician perform?"

He ignored his uncle's sarcasm, rising to leave the room before he could change his mind. Damian hadn't gone far when he was stopped by a servant with a missive addressed to him.

The flare of joy that shot through him at the sight of Pru's name scrawled across the bottom was alarming. At what point had he become so enamored with the goody-two-shoes from the neighboring estate?

He shoved the question aside for another day because she wanted to see him.

Alone.

He raced toward the thicket of trees that divided the property, not even needing exact directions to know where she'd be hiding. It was the fallen log that had played a role in any number of their childish games.

Well, *his* games. She'd never wanted to play. She'd been too busy with her lessons or trying and failing to keep her pinafore perfectly crisp and clean.

Now he knew why, of course, but at the time all he'd wanted to do was make a mess of her starched white fabric and tug her long braids until she lost that fearsome scowl.

And now... Well, now she'd lost the scowl and he found he wanted it back. He far preferred an angry sanctimonious impossibly prudent Pru to one who cowered in fear.

When he spotted her, pacing the area between the two trees that formed a sort of gateway between the properties, he was fairly certain his heart stopped. His blood burned in his veins.

Whatever this was, this new reaction to seeing Prudence, he wasn't certain he liked it and he had no idea what to do about it.

"Damian!" She cried out his name so sweetly when she saw him. Almost like she'd missed him. The thought warmed his heart. It also made him realize that he *had* missed her. Which was ridiculous. He'd seen her less than twenty-four hours before.

"Damian, what are we to do?" she asked as he drew near.

He stared down at her for a moment, only now seeing the panic in her eyes. And then it hit him.

Of course.

The reality of her situation was only now occurring to her. She couldn't have spent an evening with that pompous bore and not seen the writing on the wall.

She wasn't meant for a man like that. A man like Mr. Benedict would stifle her. He would bring out her worst tendencies and smother the parts of her that made her so deliciously Pru. Her passion, her straightforwardness, her vulnerability and her clever methods of hiding it, her big heart, and her even bigger brain...

"Damian, are you even listening to me?"

Her wonderful tendency to sigh as she talked as though she could hardly contain her exasperation for one more moment.

His lips curved up at the thought. "My apologies, what were you saying? You wish to avoid this engagement, of course, but—"

"What? No! Of course I don't want out of the agreement."

He found himself gaping like she'd been staring at him. As though she'd just grown a second head. "You don't?"

She looked pained at the very idea. "Of course not! Why would you think such a thing?"

Why? He shifted uncomfortably, watching as the breeze stirred the dark locks near her temple and pressed the too-loose gown against the lovely curves of her body.

Why indeed?

She'd never show the slightest interest in abandoning this union, only in making it a certainty. That was what these lessons were all about. He rubbed at his forehead in confusion. At what point had he lost track of that?

He supposed it was because up until yesterday afternoon her potential husband had been invisible. Unthreatening. Now he was a dark cloud looming overhead, threatening to wreak havoc and impossible to ignore.

But at this particular moment she seemed less bothered by the doom of her future than by him. Her glare turned fiery. "Are you even listening to me at all?"

He tugged at his cravat as it hit him with full force. She would marry Mr. Benedict. She wanted to marry that man.

Had it suddenly grown uncomfortably warm out here? Why was it so beastly hot on an autumn afternoon like this? His insides felt like they might combust. Perhaps something had gone sour in his breakfast because that was the only explanation for this sudden churning in his gut whenever he thought of Prudence and that doughy-faced bore with the blank stare.

Prudence threw her hands up, her eyes wide. "What are we going to do?"

"About what?"

"About me? *Performing*." She hissed the word 'performing' like it was a scandalous act.

"What are you worried about? You needn't play the pianoforte. I'd be happy to accompany you."

"You want me to *sing*?" Her voice went up so high he winced.

"I take it you do not relish the idea of singing." He'd aimed for droll but fell short.

Her answer was a glare. "You had better not be finding this amusing. After all, your reputation as a musical genius is at stake here, remember."

"I remember." He tried not to smile, he truly did. But the way she'd said 'musical genius' made it impossible.

She jabbed a finger into his chest. "You are not allowed to be amused."

Without thinking, he placed a hand over hers and held it to him. All at once the atmosphere between them shifted from her bickering exasperation and his answering amusement to something else entirely.

This 'something' seemed to crackle in the air between them and weigh him down like he was moving in the midst of a dense, thick fog.

"What are you doing?" Her words sounded muted, her lips barely moving.

He knew this because he couldn't seem to drag his gaze away from those lips.

So many emotions chasing each other like a dog chasing its tail. There were thoughts and feelings and emotions he'd never once felt before and knew not how to name. There were so many things he wanted to say. But what came out of his mouth was, "You don't really care if you impress this stuck-up bore, do you?"

"How do you know he's a stuck-up bore?" she returned.

He tugged her closer and she didn't resist. His heart was pounding, his blood roaring in his ears. "You didn't deny it."

"Because it doesn't matter if he's a bore or not." Her words were even but her breathlessness gave her away. She wasn't as unmoved by his proximity as her words made it seem. "He is the man I am to wed."

"Is that what you wish?" He found himself holding his breath.

"It is what I've been meant for my whole life."

"And I'm meant to be a marquess," he said. "But I do not wish it. So I'm asking you again, do you wish to marry that man who you've only just met?"

She blinked, her brows drawing together as if the question confused her. "I have no other options. If I do not marry him..." She didn't finish. Jerking her hand away, her eyes flashed, her chin set. Her shoulders straightened with resolve.

He saw the moment she convinced herself that she had no other option and so she would embrace this one.

"Pru, you are the one who told me that I could make of my life what I wished. Why should it not be the same for you?"

She arched her brows. "Do you honestly believe that? With my parentage and the scandal and—"

"I come from a scandal too, you might recall."

Her eyes flashed again, and this time it was with bitter anger. "You think that the fortunes and fate of an heir presumptive to a marquess is the same as that of a scandalous daughter with very few connections and a modest dowry?" She took a step back, irritation clear in her gaze.

"Do you honestly think we are the same? That our options are similar?"

He hated the resignation in her eyes. He hated it even more that she was pulling away from him, crushing the intimacy of this moment. "Pru..." He drew her name out as he moved toward her, unwilling to let her walk away. And once again he knew not what he wished to say. All he knew was that he couldn't let this moment end without telling her how he felt.

And how is that?

He swallowed a thickness in his throat. A painful ache in his chest. He wasn't sure what this was, but he didn't want it to end.

And he certainly couldn't stand by and watch her marry someone so clearly beneath her in personality and charm and grace and—

"What are you doing?" she snapped.

He stopped. He hadn't realized he'd been following her, stalking her like prey as she backpedaled away from him.

While he felt like he was drowning in the fierce intensity of these new feelings, she looked like she might scatter into the wind if he touched her wrong. Her whole body seemed to vibrate with tension and for a moment he feared she might shatter. Her eyes were darting this way and that, her feet shuffling backwards.

He had a horrible feeling she was getting ready to bolt.

"What if there were other options, what if—"

Her wide-eyed look temporarily stopped him. Her shock looked horrifyingly similar to...horror.

Nerves had his mouth going dry. Was he really doing this? Was he honestly suggesting she turn her nose on the life she'd planned? And for what? For him? For a man with a bad reputation, whose prospects for the future were a gamble, at best?

THE MISGIVINGS ABOUT MISS PRUDENCE

Was that what he was asking?

Yes. He reached for her hands and held them tight. *Yes, he was.*

"What if there was someone else," he started, his voice gruffer than he'd ever heard it as the enormity of his emotions overtook him like a tidal wave. His head was reeling. When had this happened? At what point had Prudence gone from being the bane of his existence to the center of it? When had her happiness begun to mean more to him than his own?

When exactly had he lost all reason and fallen head over heels in love with Pru?

As his thoughts threatened to run away from him, Pru actually did.

She tugged her hands out of his grip and stumbled back a few steps. He was shocked to see tears welling in her eyes. The sight of them clawed at his heart.

"Pru, what I'm trying to say is, there is someone else."

She shook her head before he could continue. "This is what my aunt wants—"

"But what about what *you* want?" Frustration made his tone harsh and for once he was the one glowering as they faced off. "What about what *I* want?"

She shook her head again, quicker this time, her brows drawn together in consternation. "I don't know...I can't believe that..." She took a deep breath and seemed to pull herself together through sheer strength. Her chin tilted up in stubborn defiance.

He'd grown to love that look but right now it made him cold. He knew what she would say before she even said it.

"It does not matter what I want," she said. Her back was straight, her lips pinched.

He took a step toward her but she moved back quickly

before turning to rush off toward her home and her aunt and the future that she did not want but would not defy.

Of course she wouldn't. This was Pru. Loyal and obedient to a fault.

Except when she was with him.

A sharp pain in his chest had him bending over at the waist, resting his hands on his knees. He'd known she wouldn't let something so silly as emotions cloud her judgement. When it came to making decisions, his Pru would always choose honor and loyalty and duty over her own wants and desires.

He closed his eyes and let out a huff of air, a humorless laugh. He'd known how this would end even as he'd started to talk. He also knew why. Her parents had made the selfish choice, and she would never make the same mistake.

It was understandable, just like his experience as a boy living outside of society had made him wary of entering back into the fold. In that sense, they were the same. Each so determined not to repeat their parents' mistakes.

Just as he knew what her response would be to any talk of this new connection they shared, he also knew that she would never be happy living the life her aunt had set out for her. But now that begged the question...at what point had he come to know Pru better than she knew herself?

And more importantly, how could he make her see that her quest to please her aunt was in vain? That no matter how perfectly she acted, no matter how good, how quick, how smart, she would never find the happiness there that she deserved?

He closed his eyes as he straightened, heading back toward his own home to get ready for the evening to come.

His heart felt like a dead weight but his mind was clearer now than it ever had been before.

He loved Prudence Pottermouth. And for better or worse, he was going to make sure she knew it.

But first...

A smile tugged at his lips.

First he would make sure that her performance tonight was a success.

13

This night was destined to be a disaster. *She* would be a failure. The entire idea was ludicrous, and it was all Damian's fault.

Prudence paced the small quarters of the music room as the clocked seemed to count down to her certain doom.

She huffed loudly at the thought. See what he'd done? Damian's grand plan had her so off kilter she was starting to have the sort of melodramatic thoughts befitting Louisa.

That would not do.

She forced herself to sit primly on a settee and take deep, even breaths.

She would not turn into Louisa. No, sir. No matter what the situation, she had her head on her shoulders and she would survive with her pride and dignity intact.

She shut her eyes tight at the thought of the horror to come.

Fine, perhaps she would not survive with her dignity, but she *would* survive. And whatever the extent of Aunt Eleanor's wrath, she would survive it. There was no other option.

What if there were other options? What if there was someone else?

She clenched her hands into fists and screwed her eyes shut so tightly it hurt. She could not go there. The memory of those few brief moments when he'd touched her...when he'd held her hands and made her believe...

She gave her head a quick jarring shake. He'd gone crazy, that was the only explanation for the way he'd looked at her, the way he'd held her close.

And she was just as insane, obviously. Because she'd let him hold her, and when he'd hinted that maybe there could be a future for them, well...

She stood up abruptly.

Obviously there could be no such thing. He was the heir to a marquess. He could have any lady he wanted. More importantly, he'd never even *liked* her and she'd never cared for him, either. She bit her lip. She'd never cared for him...until recently.

But what he was saying, what he was inferring—it was just Damian being Damian. He was reckless, impulsive. More than that, he was kind.

She let out a loud exhale as she sank back down into her seat. Her bones suddenly felt like heavy rocks and her whole body seemed to tremble with the weight of this new realization.

He was *kind*. Even as a child when he was forever teasing and playing pranks, he'd always been kind. He had a good heart. And she had no doubt it was that kindness that had led to his rash actions earlier.

Or at least, she'd assumed he was hinting that *he* was another option.

She rubbed at her temples as she replayed everything he'd said, every look, every touch...

Surely that was what he'd meant, but it was best to forget

it immediately because he'd been taking pity, maybe even hoping to save the poor fool who'd gone and fallen for him.

Her groan sounded loud in the vacant room.

Was that what this was, this muddled mix of emotions? Was this what it meant to have...feelings for someone?

She clapped a hand over her chest and rubbed where her chest ached. Then she supposed it was no wonder all of her friends had fallen victim. This illness was overwhelming in its attack and brutal with its symptoms.

At this particular moment she could even understand why her parents had chosen as they had. They'd been in love.

But they'd also been selfish.

She opened her eyes slowly this time, letting the room come into focus as she evened her breathing and blocked out the memories that threatened to drown her. Damian dancing with her; Damian being patient and kind no matter how many times she fumbled over the keys; Damian teasing her and making her laugh; Damian looking at her and seeing her and...

And liking what he saw.

The realization was so sweet it brought tears to her eyes.

"There you are." Aunt Eleanor marched into the room looking put out already. "Are you hiding, child?"

"No, Aunt Eleanor." She came to stand just as voices filled the hallway. Aunt Eleanor's voice dropped to a whisper that was all the more terrifying for its softness. "Mr. Benedict is your only chance, girl, and don't you forget it. After everything I've done for you, you had better make this match, or else."

Pru blinked. She had no idea what 'or else' meant in this context but she could guess. Her aunt would wash her hands of her once and for all, no doubt. Her only family would abandon her...again.

"I understand, Aunt Eleanor."

Her aunt grunted in acknowledgment.

"Pardon the interruption..." Damian swept into the room so quickly, his voice so loud it made her stiffen. He flashed her a small smile before turning a far more elegant grin in the direction of her aunt, charming her with small talk and questions about the elderly lady's health.

Pru took the opportunity to watch him. There he was, the consummate charmer. The heir to a marquess. The golden boy who lived life dangerously, led by his heart and his soul and his passion.

She caught a pathetic little sigh before it could escape.

Oh yes, Damian's appeal was undeniable, but her aunt was right. He was not for her. Even if he felt this way for her. Even if it wasn't just kindness and pity on his part...

Choosing her would be selfish on his part.

Choosing him would be even more selfish on her part.

"And so, if you'll excuse us," he was saying to her aunt with a wave of his hand that seemed to include Prudence. "I'd like a word with my protege before the recital begins."

The recital.

How had she managed to forget that in mere moments her world would come to a crushing, brutal, humiliating end?

Drat. She truly was turning into Louisa. Perhaps love made everyone dramatic.

Her aunt gave them space. Not so much that they could repeat the incident that occurred earlier today, but enough so that they could speak privately in hushed voices.

"We didn't finish our talk earlier," he said the moment her aunt had reached the far side of the room to loudly criticize the flower arrangement. A nearby maid looked ready to cry.

That girl wouldn't last in this household for long if she couldn't handle being yelled at.

She couldn't bring herself to look directly at Damian. It

was easier to watch the poor girl tremble than to face the tenderness and affection she feared she might see when she looked to Damian.

"Pru, look at me."

She huffed, pursing her lips as she tried to feel annoyed with him for his heavy handedness. "I do not know why you got me into this in the first place," she said when she finally dragged her gaze upward to look at him.

His lips twitched with amusement. "You couldn't avoid this forever, you know."

For a moment she wasn't sure to what he was referring. To this moment right here and now? To her potential marriage? To another dreaded recital?

It didn't matter.

"I'm not ready," she hissed.

"Of course you are." For once there was no laughter in his eyes, no twitch to his lips. He was serious. "You are Prudence Pottermouth, the strongest, bravest girl I know."

She tried to think of a way to snap at him, to chide him or glare at him...but she couldn't. Her lips were trembling too much to purse, tears were pricking the back of her eyes, and her heart...

Her heart felt as though it was breaking. The way he was looking at her right now, with such confidence and admiration, with such tenderness and...and *love*.

It made her want to laugh and weep and scream all at once.

Instead she turned away. Her gaze moved toward the door where the small crowd of soon-to-be-horrified audience members were talking amongst themselves. The marquess seemed to be the center of attention and she watched in horror as her potential fiancé fawned over the man like he was the prince regent himself.

"I can't go through with this." The whisper escaped before

she could stop it. She wasn't even certain herself to what she was referring. Watching this man—this bore—this would-be gentleman who cared not for her intellect nor her company, but who was merely in the market for a show horse. Someone with the right connections he could trot out at gatherings to impress his colleagues.

She pressed a hand to her belly. No, she could not do this.

"You can." Damian murmured the words of encouragement gently. "I did not lie to your aunt when I said that you were ready."

"You told her I was perfect," she hissed, latching on to anger and her fears of performing in front of an audience because it was easier than thinking about what else was to come. The stand she must take. The decision that had been made in her heart that could not be undone.

"Music is not meant to be perfect," he said, his voice low but insistent. His gaze held hers, so fierce. So kind. So understanding. "It is meant to be filled with emotion, which you have. It is meant to encompass passion and beauty and elegance." He leaned forward, so close that his lips brushed against the wisps of hair at her temple. "And that is all you, my dear."

She shut her eyes as if that could shut out the words. "You know what I mean, Damian. Now they expect me to be good. To be *perfect*."

"And you are perfect."

Her eyes snapped open and she found herself looking straight into her worst fear. Love.

"You are perfect to me," he said. His fingers touched her chin, tilting her face up so she was forced to see the emotions there.

Her heart leapt into her throat at the sight of it, at once so eerily familiar and so disconcertingly strange.

"Just keep your eyes on me," he said. No, he commanded.

Her brows arched in surprise at his tone and his lips quirked. "Just this once, Pru, do as I say. Yes?"

She nodded and even managed to add, "I suppose I must. You *are* the musical genius."

His low rumble of laughter warmed her all the way through and eased the tension that had been choking her throat and making her rib cage feel too tight.

"This is as simple as singing a hymn at church, which you did beautifully as a child."

She opened her mouth to protest but he held up a finger to stop her.

"And today will be no different. Do not try to be anything other than who you are, Prudence, and you will be perfect."

She swallowed down the last of her protest and gave him a short nod instead.

Her aunt was shooing the small audience to their seats and Prudence moved so Damian could take his seat at the pianoforte. As he passed her, he paused. "And Prudence?"

"Yes?" She looked up and her heart thudded wildly at the heat in his eyes.

"When this is all over, you and I..." He leaned in closer. "We will talk."

She swallowed.

"We will finish the conversation we started today."

It wasn't a question so she did not answer. She merely watched him walk away.

When at last the dreaded recital got underway, she did as Damian instructed. She watched his fingers move over the keys so effortlessly, the way he walked through life. She kept her eyes on his soft smile that seemed to say everything would be fine.

And it would. For him, it would.

She watched his eyes, which were the first eyes to ever

look at her as though he saw her—completely and in all her imperfect glory—and found her loveable nonetheless.

And when it came time for her to open her mouth and sing, the sight of him staring back at her, that smile and his gaze—it relaxed her enough to get through the song.

Not perfectly. Very far from perfectly.

But she savored the moment all the same.

* * *

WHILE THE MARQUESS was cornered by Mr. Benedict, Aunt Eleanor was having a quiet conversation in the far corner with Sir William, that left Pru and Damian on their own.

Alone...except for all the other people in the room.

They might as well have been alone, though. To her mind, there was no one else there.

"You were amazing tonight," Damian said.

She laughed. "I was passable."

"You were perfect."

She rolled her eyes. "You were the only person to think so."

He narrowed his eyes as if mulling it over. "Everyone else is a dullard."

She let out an utterly unladylike snort of amusement. "If you say so."

He puffed his chest out. "Well, I am the musical genius here. And I do say so."

She tipped her chin to concede. "I will not argue the point. If the musical genius says I was perfect, who am I to fight it?"

He laughed at the teasing in her tone like she'd hoped he would.

She truly hadn't been all that good, but she'd held a tune,

all thanks to him. Her gaze hadn't wavered from him, though it was likely rude to ignore the audience.

But with her eyes on him and his on her, she'd been able to relax. To be herself. And whether her aunt had approved...she knew not.

She doubted it.

She was almost guaranteed to have been disappointed.

But even so, Prudence would survive. Just like she would survive whatever retribution came her way when she informed her aunt that she would not marry Mr. Benedict. She couldn't, not when she knew for certain that it would be more of the same. She'd always thought marriage would spare her from the miserable life she'd had with her great aunt, unappreciated, unvalued, and unloved.

But if she were to marry Mr. Benedict, it would be more of the same. And the thought of it, a lifetime sentence of more of the same...

She could not do it. It was no longer a matter of what she wished or what she wanted, it was now a matter of what she could bear.

She might not be able to have the man who'd stolen her heart, but she could not bear to commit the rest of her life to more of the same. She'd rather face the fear of an unknown future than the certainty of crushing disappointment.

Now she just had to tell Mr. Benedict.

And her great aunt.

Her stomach roiled at the thought but she shoved it to the side. For tonight, for just a little while, she wanted to be happy. Was that so much to ask?

"Pru..." Damian's voice instantly set her on edge, so filled with meaning. "We need to talk."

She looked away to make sure no one overheard. She supposed he was right. So much had happened between them, and yet...nothing at all.

He hadn't compromised her, and she was still promised to another. Or at least she assumed that was the conversation happening right now on the other end of the room.

She wouldn't be for long, but Damian needn't know that. Because if he did, if he thought for one moment that her crying off this potential engagement was because of him…

She winced as she remembered what he'd said only the day before about wanting to save her.

He would, that was the beautiful thing about Damian. The thing she hadn't noticed when she'd been young, or at least she hadn't been charitable enough to give him credit for.

He was protective and generous and thoughtful. A tease and a prankster and a rebel…and good. He was such a good man.

So good that he would anger his uncle and thwart all of society just to save her from an unhappy marriage.

The thought made her breathing shaky.

He was so kind that he would feel the need to take care of her, maybe even marry her if he knew that what she felt for him was what was finally setting her free.

Terror the likes of which she'd never known had her closing her eyes for a moment. But this terror wasn't enough to shake her resolve.

Damian had opened her eyes to the fact that she'd been living in fear for far too long. She'd spent a lifetime trying to fit into a role that was too small. She'd worked her whole life to be the perfect niece and one evening in Mr. Benedict's presence and she'd known that her future would be more of the same.

"Prudence?" Damian's voice was soft. Gentle. "Are you all right?"

She forced a smile. "Yes," she said.

She would be. Of that she was certain.

His gaze was warm and knowing. "It will be all right, you'll see. I'll make certain of it."

Her smile trembled. That was the trouble. He would make everything all right if she let him, but she couldn't allow that.

He had a life ahead of him, one filled with obligations and duties that he could not shirk. His uncle would never approve of her, and society as a whole would have a fit. A marquess could not marry the daughter of a scandal. A gently bred woman, yes, but her connections were not outstanding and besides all that, she knew as well as he that it would be a union born of pity.

Sympathy.

Kindness.

That was nothing to ruin a life over, and she couldn't bear to be the cause of his downfall. He'd weathered his parents' scandal and that was all he ought to bear.

He might not see it yet, but being selfish never led to any good and if she let him help her, she would be making the most selfish choice of all.

Her aunt and Sir William started to head their way.

"Meet me tomorrow," Damian murmured under his breath. "Promise me."

She nodded. It was the best she could do.

She never had been much good at lying.

14

*D*amian stared at the miserable-looking lady's maid who'd acted as chaperone merely two days before. "What do you mean, she is gone?"

Her sigh was filled with impatience. "I apologize, my lord, but she is not here."

He gave his head a little shake and scrubbed a hand over his eyes. There had to be some sort of miscommunication here. "Where did she go? Into town?" He was already half turning toward the stables where he'd left his horse, too eager to get to Prudence this morning to walk the distance between properties.

"She's gone back to London." It was the Dowager Demon's voice in the hallway that made him freeze.

"London?" He turned back slowly and found himself facing that frightening smile as the old lady stalked toward him.

"Indeed."

"When..." He cleared his throat, trying to ignore the panicky sensation setting in. "When did she leave?"

"First light of dawn." Her tone was so brisk as though her

words weren't crushing him where he stood. "She should be back to that silly school of hers soon enough, I'd imagine, though what she plans to do with herself once she wears out her welcome there, I have no idea."

His mouth parted as he gaped at the old woman who seemed to be shooing him toward the door as she spoke. "What do you mean?"

The dowager duchess's mouth turned hard. Cruel. Unforgiving. "I mean, she made her bed when she refused Mr. Benedict. Now she must lie in it."

His heart was galloping. His blood rushing past his ears in a roar as he struggled to keep up. All he could think was—she refused him! His Pru had refused him!

He gave his head a shake as the ramifications hit. Her aunt was cruel at the best of times, but if Pru had gone against her wishes, thrown away the alliance her great aunt set in place—no doubt for mercenary reasons on her own...

His stomach sank. Oh, his poor Pru.

She needed him now more than ever. "You ought to have let her see me," he snapped.

The older woman's eyes widened in shock. No doubt it had been a good many years since anyone had spoken to her in that tone.

He found he couldn't care in the slightest if she was offended or not.

"Ah, now I see," the dowager duchess said with a pale imitation of a smile. "The silly brat went and fell in love with you then, did she?" She sniffed in a manner he knew well—but it was far less endearing coming from this witch. "I should have known she was just like her mother. No sense, that one, no matter how much I tried to get it through to her that she was useless. Worth nothing but what value I gave her."

His hands clenched, his jaw so tight he thought it might shatter.

Never in his life had he thought he'd see the day when he itched to strike a woman. Instead, he forced words out through clenched teeth. "She is worth more than a heartless lady like you could ever imagine."

She froze in shock, her lady's maid tensing beside her with wide eyes. The dowager duchess shocked them both when she let out a bark of a laugh in response. "So you're just as much of a fool as she is, I see." Her laughter was cold and harsh. "Perhaps you two would have made a fine pair." She shook her head, disgust plain as day on her features. "Two selfish brats, no better than their good-for-nothing parents."

He let the insults slide off him. All that mattered now was finding Pru. He needed to make sure she was all right and then make this right.

He straightened to his full height and summoned every ounce of training his uncle had instilled in him for the day he inherited the title. "I'm going to retrieve your niece now, and when I get back, my wife will expect an apology."

The old woman had the nerve to scoff and when she next spoke she had the sort of smug cruelty of a predator toying with its prey. "I wish you luck, I assure you. But I don't know what makes you think that headstrong little brat will be any more reasonable for you than me. After all, I told her she ought to see you to formally apologize for embarrassing you with her poor performance the other night."

His stomach sank as the dowager duchess's eyes lit with malice. He could see it coming clearly, whatever it was this old witch was holding over him.

"Even this morning, I told her she was free to make a stop at your estate to leave a note formally apologizing and to say her goodbyes…"

His heart twisted in his chest.

"But I'm afraid Prudence didn't wish to see you." Her smile morphed into a sneer as she shut the door in his face. "And neither do I."

* * *

His uncle was no help whatsoever. "If she left of her own volition, I'm not sure what you can do about it."

"But Uncle..." Damian dropped his head back with a groan. "I was going to propose."

"I know, and I already told you that I believed it was a poor decision." His uncle's expression was wary, as it had been the night before when Damian first told his uncle of his plan.

He hadn't exactly been seeking permission, but his uncle had granted it all the same—along with a word of warning about marrying for all the wrong reasons.

Namely, love.

"Look, Uncle Edward, I know you had a bad experience, but that doesn't mean that I cannot make this work."

His uncle leaned back in his seat with a sigh. "It's just..." He sighed again and shifted, eyeing Damian carefully. "You are young and so is she. It's easy to confuse longing with love at your age and—"

"I love her, Uncle. Of that I am certain." Even as he said it, the words felt right. There was no other word for it. Did he long for her? Certainly. Did he find her beautiful and enchanting?

Of course.

But it was more than that. He loved the way her mind worked; he loved that he was one of few who was lucky enough to see past her prim, pursed lips and her fierce scowls to the sweet, vulnerable, giant heart that lay beneath.

He loved that she challenged him and that she saw

straight through his charm and his flirtation to the man beneath. He loved that she did not laugh at his dreams of a conservatory and that she saw all that he wished he could be.

He loved...*her*. He loved her with all his heart, and he knew that she felt the same.

"Are you certain that she shares your feelings?" his uncle asked.

"Yes." He said it without a doubt because if there was one thing he knew it was Prudence. And there was no denying the emotions he'd seen in her eyes when they'd been alone together. There was no way he'd been alone when the very real, very physical connection pulled them together and seemed to wrap them in a cocoon of their very own.

He stopped pacing his uncle's office long enough to turn and face him. "I know that she feels it, too."

His uncle looked like he wished to argue, but he merely nodded. "Very well, then. I suppose there's only one thing left to do."

Damian was already heading toward the door. "I can be in London by nightfall."

"Good luck," his uncle called after him.

His head was spinning as he mounted his ride. He had no time to prepare for a journey, not when the woman he loved was on her own, no doubt terrified about what the future had in store.

Why had she left like that? Why hadn't she come to him?

He shook off the fears that threatened to mar his certainty. He would go to her, he would find her. And once he did...

He wouldn't leave her side until she agreed to be his bride.

15

Delilah was watching her warily as she and the other girls pretended to embroider. "So you just...left, then?"

Prudence, who actually *was* embroidering, continued to stare at the linen in her hands. "That is correct."

"Well..." Delilah's voice trailed off in what was either shock or awe or perhaps a mix of the two.

Prudence didn't have to look up and see Delilah's expression to know that she'd stunned her best friend. She'd stunned herself with her rash actions.

"Well, I for one am proud of you," Louisa said, leaning over to wrap an arm around her shoulders in a side hug.

"Yes, yes, of course," Delilah said quickly. "I am so very proud of you for standing up to that nasty great aunt of yours. It's just so surprising, that's all."

"Very surprising," Addie added as she bounced her brother Reggie on her knee.

It was Miss Grayson who broke the silence and asked the one question she did not wish to face. "Do you have any idea what you will do now?"

Her hands froze over the embroidery. She'd been doing nothing but think about that ever since she'd left her aunt's house. The entire carriage ride back to town had been filled with that question.

Well, that wasn't quite true. The ride back she'd dwelled extensively on the dilemma of what she would do now that her aunt had washed her hands of her and the last of her family saw her as a disgrace, that was true.

But what she studiously *hadn't* thought about had seemed to fill that long carriage ride even more.

A particular person.

And unwanted feelings.

She dropped her linen into her lap with a sigh. "I have no idea what I shall do, but I won't be a burden to you any longer than I have to."

Miss Grayson leaned forward and laid a hand over hers. "You could never be a burden, dear Prudence. You are a part of this family, and you always will be."

Prudence was horrified to find tears welling in her eyes at the kindness. It was hardly unexpected—Miss Grayson was always kind. She was the kindest woman Prudence knew, and the most sensible as well. And as if that wasn't enough, Miss Grayson was a beauty and no one could deny it.

And yet she was nearly on the shelf.

And Prudence was sure to follow. She glanced down at her frumpy gown and her too large hips. She did not need a mirror to see that she was plain—too plain for the likes of Damian.

He'd see that one day, and when he did...well, she did not wish to be there as a witness.

"Perhaps you could tell us more of this music tutor you spoke of in your letters," Delilah said.

Prudence sniffed, her lips pressing together in a scowl

that felt too familiar. "Really, Delilah, subtlety is not your specialty."

Delilah grinned, utterly unrepentant. "So Rupert tells me. But it's still amusing to play coy."

Addie laughed and Louisa leaned forward. "I've heard Lord Damian is exceedingly handsome, is that true?"

Prudence sniffed. "I wouldn't know."

"What?" Addie laughed again. "You do not have eyes?"

"Of course I have eyes," she said, her tone turning smug and sanctimonious.

Heavens, had she always sounded so much like Mr. Benedict? How did any of her friends stand her?

And yet she couldn't seem to shake it. She fell back into her role of priggish Pru with ease. It was safer this way. This was far more comfortable than the Prudence she'd become these past weeks while away.

Still the same but...different. Uncovered. Laid bare.

And all because a rakish young gentleman had decided to flirt with her and make her laugh. She picked up her embroidery just so she could have the satisfaction of stabbing something.

"So?" Louisa asked, all impatience and frenetic energy, as always. "Is he as handsome as they say or not?"

"He is very handsome." Her lips felt numb. She didn't wish to speak of Damian. She didn't wish to think about him or hear about him or—

"Miss Grayson, there is a visitor." The housekeeper looked flustered as she entered the room, and it was no wonder. It was far too late for visitors.

"I'll be back in a moment," Miss Grayson said before sweeping out of the room. So graceful, their Miss Grayson. So perfectly perfect.

Prudence stabbed at her embroidery again.

Aunt Eleanor would have loved to have a great niece like Miss Grayson.

"Come on, then," Delilah said, pulling the embroidery out of her hands before she could destroy it. "It is just us girls. You can tell us."

She feigned surprise. "Tell you what?"

All three of them exchanged looks that made her want to scream. Like an outsider looking in, as always, but this was worse than ever because they looked so sympathetic. So understanding.

"You have feelings for him, don't you?" Addie asked gently.

And that was the worst of it. They did understand.

She shook her head but couldn't bring herself to voice the lie.

"Oh dear, you can talk to us." Delilah gave her a sympathetic smile as she placed a hand over hers. "If anyone understands how confusing love can be, it's us."

She looked from one sweet, gentle smile to the next. Yes, they did understand...but they also had no idea.

Because their love was reciprocated. Hers was not. It could not be.

So she tugged her hand out from beneath Delilah's. "This is not the same thing at all."

Miss Grayson reentered the room as Louisa came to sit beside her on the settee. "Then try explaining it to us."

Prudence shook her head, her throat growing tight with their kindness. "I cannot explain it to you, none of you would understand."

Miss Grayson cleared her throat softly in the doorway. "Then perhaps you ought to explain it to Lord Damian."

Prudence blinked in surprise. "Pardon me?"

Miss Grayson's wince spoke of sympathy and regret...and perhaps just a twinge of amusement. She nodded toward the entryway. "He is here and he wishes to see you."

* * *

PRUDENCE'S HANDS were shaking as she left her friends in the warm comfort of the private sitting room and made her way toward the formal drawing room, with Miss Grayson by her side.

"Will you be all right, dear?" Miss Grayson asked quietly when Prudence's steps grew slower with each passing second.

She nodded but her mouth was too dry to reply.

"I'll keep the door open, but I'll give you some privacy, shall I?" Miss Grayson asked. She didn't seem to be waiting for an answer as she nudged her into the room and poked her head through the doorway behind her. "I'll be just out here in the hall should you need me."

Miss Grayson might have said more, but if she did, Prudence didn't hear it. She was too busy gaping at the sight before her.

Damian had never been so handsome. Nor such a mess. He hadn't bothered to wash the dirt of travel off of himself or even shave, it seemed.

He looked...well, he looked like a ruffian. But that somehow made him that much more handsome. Like some dastardly highwayman come straight off the pages of one of Louisa's gothic romances.

"You're well," he said. He seemed to be speaking to himself as his gaze traveled over her, taking in every detail of her plain gown and her simple updo as she was scrutinizing him.

She was surprised to see his shoulders slump in relief.

He'd truly been worried about her welfare.

That knowledge jarred her out of her shock long enough to assure him. "I am fine. Thank you for your concern."

He nodded, his expression inscrutable and his gaze fierce. "I am glad. I was worried when you left so quickly."

Her gaze dropped to the ground as shame washed through her. He'd worried about her. Of course he had, he was kind like that. She hadn't meant to alarm him, only protect herself.

"I suppose your aunt shipped you off too quickly for you to come and say goodbye," he said, his tone holding a question and...something else. There was an edge there she'd never heard before.

Was he angry? Upset? She glanced up and swallowed thickly at the dark intensity of his gaze.

"Uh…" She meant to agree. It would be simple enough to blame her aunt for her hasty departure. But she'd never been good at lying, particularly not to him. "I did not wish to see you."

Guilt slammed into her, making her drop her gaze again in shame. What a coward. So weak in the face of her emotions. She'd known that if she'd seen him, if he'd been kind and taken pity…

She wouldn't have been able to walk away. She cleared her throat. "I did not want to say goodbye."

"I know." His voice was clipped.

Her head snapped up as she faced him. "You do?"

"Your aunt told me so, but I supposed I'd hoped that she was lying." He shrugged, his smile rueful and sad. "I wouldn't put it past her to lie to me if she thought it would inflict pain."

She made a noncommittal sound of agreement.

He titled his head to the side as if to see her better. "From your aunt, I'd expect to be hurt. I did not see it coming from you, however."

Prudence winced. "I-I'm sorry. I didn't mean to hurt your feelings—"

"Then why did you leave without a word?" He let out a huff of air and ran a hand through his hair. When he spoke next he softened his voice. "Why, Pru? Was it because..." He licked his lips and shifted his stance as if bracing himself. "Was it because you knew what I was going to say? Did you suspect that I would propose?"

She saw the hurt in his eyes and it made her own ache intensify a millionfold. But she couldn't lie. "Yes," she whispered.

He flinched and closed his eyes briefly. "And you thought that it would be easier to avoid the conversation altogether than to reject me."

It wasn't a question, but still she said, "Yes."

He stared at her for a long, excruciatingly quiet moment. Then he shook his head slowly, his brows coming down in confusion. "Why?"

She blinked in surprise. Wasn't it obvious?

She blinked again when his expression shifted from confusion to suspicion and he took a giant stride in her direction, closing the gap so thoroughly that she could not breathe.

Well, she could, but she didn't wish to. If she were to inhale his scent, feel his warmth...

She didn't trust herself to be strong. But she needed to be, for his sake.

He leaned in close, his eyes peering at her as though she were a science experiment. "Why, Pru? Why would you say no when I know for certain that you love me?"

16

As far as proposals went, this was not exactly what he'd had in mind. Damian hadn't spent much time daydreaming about how he'd one day propose, but if he had, he wouldn't have guessed that it would be like this.

Demanding the woman he loved to admit that she loved him back.

But now that the word 'love' was out there, and his gamble paid off because the look in her eyes…

It said everything.

He'd been right. Her shock, her horror… While they were hardly flattering—horror was not the first emotion he'd hoped to see during his proposal—they were the affirmation he needed. Rudely jabbing a finger in her direction, he couldn't help but crow, "I knew it."

She jerked back as if he'd struck her. "You…what?"

"I knew you loved me." He stalked toward her. If she thought he was going to let her run away again, she could think again.

"I-I didn't say that," she said.

"But you do."

She glared.

He grinned.

This was more like it. "Why did you run, Pru? Why did you leave without a goodbye when you had to know that I'm in love with you, too."

His voice rose in anger as he spoke and he ended with a huff. No, that was definitely not how he'd planned to tell her that he loved her. But now that his panic over her welfare was fading, frustration was taking its place.

And, if he were being totally honest, alongside frustration there was pain. His pride was stinging and his chest still ached just as it had when he'd discovered she'd left without so much as a farewell.

"Y-you're in love with me?" she echoed. Her eyes were deliciously dazed. "But you can't be."

He frowned, his hands on his hips as he glowered at her. "And why is that?"

"Because I'm not—that is, I will never be…." She seemed to give up with a loud sigh of exasperation that was so very Pru it made his lips twitch with amusement.

Her mouth pursed and her expression became unbearably superior. So very sanctimonious. "What you feel for me isn't love, Damian."

"I beg your pardon," he interrupted.

"It's sympathy," she continued. He caught a flicker of a wince before she added, "It's pity."

"Sympathy? Pity?" His head jerked back and his voice was so loud he wouldn't be surprised if her friends rushed in to save her. Running a hand through his mussed hair, he gave his head a shake in disbelief. "You think I want to marry you out of *pity*?"

She pressed her lips together tighter. Priggish Pru in all her glory. With a little shrug, she added, "You feel sorry for me. Admit it."

He leaned in toward her, lowering his voice as he tried to contain his frustration. "You are a very difficult woman to feel sorry for, do you know that?" He started pacing to keep from reaching for her. He wanted to pull her close, to kiss her, to make her promise that she would never run from him again.

But he couldn't do any of that until he got this simple truth through her thick skull. "I do feel sorry that you were stuck with such a poor excuse for a guardian your whole life," he said, still pacing as she stood still as a statue in the center of the room. Her hands folded neatly, her face composed as she'd been taught.

"See?" Pru sniffed. "It's merely sympathy because you are a kind man."

"Kind...*kind*?"

Her brows drew together at his insensible railing, but really. *Kind?* That was all she saw in him?

She drew in a deep breath. "Yes, kind. But one day you will realize that you don't really love me and you'll regret your decision. I am not fit to be a marchioness and I am not the woman you should be tied to for the rest of your life."

He gaped at her for a long, tense moment.

"Prudence Pottermouth." He drew her name out as he moved toward her slowly. "I've called you many names over the years and have accused you of being a goody two shoes, a prudish prig, a—"

"Is there a point to this?" she snapped.

"Yes, because I never once suspected you to be a martyr."

She stiffened, her brows drawing down as she returned his glare.

"It seems I'll have to add that to your list of faults," he continued. "And yes, I am well aware of your faults, just as I suspect you are very well acquainted with mine."

She pinched her lips together tight and he could practically see her tallying a list of said faults.

"But if you'd let me continue, I was going to say that while I do feel sorry for your plight, I am not asking for your hand out of some sense of obligation. You more than anyone ought to know how much I detest duty and responsibility as a motivation."

She opened her mouth and closed it. He had her there.

"And besides, you feel sorry for me as well," he added.

"What?"

"Of course you do," he said with a wave of his hand. "I lost my parents, you lost yours. We're both pitiable to a degree."

She frowned again, looking flustered.

Flustered he could do. He was hardly calm and collected himself. He supposed being in love made flustered a common state.

"But are your feelings for me based in pity?" he asked.

She stared at him wide-eyed for a moment before shaking her head.

"Then why is it so hard for you to believe that mine aren't either?"

She took a deep breath, she opened her mouth, but to his surprise—and he suspected to *her* surprise as well—she started to cry.

Sniffling, she bit her lip, and his anger and frustration faded fast in the face of her tears. "Oh, Pru," he groaned as he closed the distance between them and tugged her into his arms. When she burrowed into him, her face nestling against his chest and her arms wrapping around his waist...he felt himself crash. His heart was no longer his and he knew it.

He'd been falling in love with her for who knew how long, but in this moment he hit rock bottom. She owned him, heart and soul. He couldn't stay angry with her because she was a part of him, whether she knew it or not.

When she pulled back to look at him she was still sniffling but her tears were easing and she swiped away the last of them with impatience. "How can you love me? My own friends can barely tolerate me and…" She pulled back to look down at herself and he could see the self-loathing, the critical judgement that came from years of emotional abuse. "You cannot love me."

His heart threatened to break in two with those words but he lifted a hand to tilt her chin up so she was forced to meet his gaze. "No, Pru, *you* cannot love you. Not yet, at least. But I hope in time you will come to see yourself the way that I see you."

Tears welled in her eyes again and her lower lip trembled.

"I see a woman who is strong and brave, clever and genuine, and who has so much love to give."

She flinched a bit, and he knew without her saying that she was fighting the words, that while she might want to believe him, she didn't.

"I know that you do not see it yet," he continued. "I know that you are struggling. But luckily for you, I can love you enough for both of us."

She gasped, her eyes widening.

"For now, at least," he amended. "But I hope that with enough time I can help you to see how amazing you truly are." He reached up a hand to stroke a stray lock back from her temple. "You've been told for so long that you must be perfect to be loved, but that is so far from the truth," he said, his voice gruff and low. "It is your imperfections that make you who you are. None of us are perfect. We're human." He forced a small smile as he wiped another tear away. "Whether you admit it or not, *you* are human."

She let out a sound that was part laugh and part exasperated huff.

He loved that sound.

His voice turned teasing as hope burned within him. He hated to see her tears but he was getting through to her and he knew it. "You are human," he repeated, leaning down until his nose brushed against hers. "And you're in love with me."

Her breath caught. He could feel her tense in his arms, their lips a breath apart.

"Admit it," he said, his command a gruff whisper.

She licked her lips and he held her tighter. When she nodded his heart threatened to burst out of his chest. "Yes, I love you."

He claimed her lips with a bruising kiss that she returned with just as much passion, just as much fervor.

Of course she did, because his Pru might act like the uptight sanctimonious snob but she was filled with more love than she even knew. His lips moved over hers as she leaned into his embrace.

She was his, and he was almost certain that she knew it.

The 'almost' was enough to give him pause and he grudgingly pulled back so he could look down into her sweet, dazed eyes. "Will you marry me, Prudence?"

She blinked a few times, her lips parting on a gasp.

"Before you answer, I need you to know that I meant it when I said that I may not be a marquess. That I hope I am not. I know that the promise of a title—"

She clapped a hand over his mouth with a huff that was so very Pru. "You cannot truly believe I would marry you for a title."

He grinned behind her hand. He hadn't. Not for a second. But it was still nice to hear. He removed her hand gently. "But you *will* marry me."

Her lips curved up at the corners and his heart leapt in response. "Are you certain this is what you want?"

He grinned as he held her so tight she was pressed against him from head to toe. "You are everything I want."

She bit her lip, her eyes dancing with a happiness that he hoped he'd see every day for the rest of their lives. "Then yes," she said with a happy sigh. "I would love to marry you."

As he kissed her they heard an explosion of noise from the foyer. Cheers and hoots and whistles surrounded them and Prudence pulled back with a laugh. "And I suppose it's time that you meet my friends."

He dropped his arms to reach for her hands. There was still so much he wanted to say, so many kisses he ached to give. But now he knew that he had the rest of his life.

"Something tells me I will love these friends of yours since they are the family you never had."

Her smile softened as her friends drew away from the doorway in a flurry of giggles and whispers. One of them had the good sense to click the door shut and give them privacy.

Prudence tipped her head to the side to study him. "You're right. My friends and Miss Grayson have been like a family to me. But you…" She smiled so sweetly his heart swelled in his chest. "You are my home."

He groaned as he pulled her close once more. Home. He'd never once thought he'd feel like he fit in anywhere well enough to call it home. But she was right. That was exactly what he had with Prudence. "Maybe your friends can wait for just a little while longer," he teased as he lowered his head.

She tilted hers back and went up on tiptoe to meet his, her lips curved up in a smile. "They can *definitely* wait."

ABOUT THE AUTHOR

MAGGIE DALLEN IS the author of more than a hundred romantic comedies in a range of genres including young adult, historical, and contemporary. An unapologetic addict of all things romance, she loves to connect with fellow avid readers. Come say hello on Facebook or Instagram!